# WHAT WE DID LAST NIGHT

The totally gripping psychological thriller

VANESSA GARBIN

THE BOOK FOLKS

Published by The Book Folks

London, 2021



This book is a work of fiction. Names, characters, businesses, organizations, places and events are either the product of the author's imagination or are used fictitiously. Any resemblance to actual persons, living or dead, events or locales is entirely coincidental. The spelling is Australian English.



ISBN 978-1-913516-01-7

www.thebookfolks.com

*For Raymond*

# Prologue

Two men and two women gather around the bed and stare down at the unmoving body in the dimly lit bedroom.

'She's dead.'

'What?'

'She can't be.'

'Why is she even… what's she even doing here?'

'It's her house, idiot.'

'You know what I bloody mean.'

'She's half-naked.'

'Oh God. Oh God, the poor love.'

'Is that blood?'

'I'm going to be sick… oh shit… this can't be happening…'

'Check her pulse again.'

'*You* do it.'

'I can't feel anything.'

'Jesus, what is wrong with you? Oh… oh my God… she's… the poor thing. She can't be dead. She just can't.'

'Pull the blankets up. Give her some dignity.'

'I didn't know it was her,' says a man, his voice strained in anguish. He shakes his head as he backs away from the body and bumps into a chest of drawers, sending knick-knacks wobbling and a pink, glittery candle tumbling to the ground. 'I didn't know… I thought it was… I thought Laura was play–'

'Let me *through*,' says another man entering the room, his voice rising in anger. 'Oh God... oh shit... get out of the way – now!'

'Give him some bloody room.'

A woman appears at the bedroom door. She stares at the body for several seconds and then makes a sound, somewhere between a groan and a gasp. Somebody flees the room. Another vomits into their hand.

'No, no, no,' wails the woman, who now kneels by the bed. She begins to sob, at first almost silent, then loud and raw, her guttural howls escaping through the half-opened bedroom window and travelling down the silvery, moonlit street. A street that will never be the same again.

Downstairs, the autumn wind slams the front door shut behind a man who stumbles as he runs across the lawn, fleeing the house as though it is burning.

Another man follows.

'What have we done?' come the aggrieved, low tones of a woman from a shadowy corner of the bedroom. 'Oh God, what have we done?'

Several minutes later, over the haunting wail of an ambulance siren, a single gunshot cracks into the night.

# 1

## *Laura*

I've got a bad feeling about tonight.

I'm not sure why.

I woke up before dawn with a racing heart and churning stomach, and since then a feeling of dread has been niggling away at me.

My husband, Nathan, had a laugh when I told him this morning over breakfast.

'Once you've had a few wines, you'll be glad we decided to have everyone over. It's going to be great,' he said, adding, 'And it's just our neighbours. It's not like we're having a big party or anything. Don't stress, okay?'

But here I am, only an hour before our guests are due to arrive, and my insides are a fluttery mess.

'Bye, Mum. Have fun tonight,' my daughter, Leni, shouts from across the street, startling me from my thoughts.

Her long golden hair catches the fiery glow of the setting sun and when she smiles, my heart nearly bursts with love and pride. She is so beautiful, inside and out, our Leni.

As I watch her turn and walk away, I wonder where the years have gone.

'I will,' I call back. 'You too. Say hi to Tristan.'

Leni is dating Samantha and Orlando's son. They've been our neighbours for years so we've known Tristan since he was a little boy.

In fact, our entire street is like one big happy family.

The front door opens behind me.

'There you are,' says Nathan.

I turn and watch him dance his way towards me with a beer in his right hand for him and a frosted glass of white in the other for me.

'Why are you so jolly?' I ask. He's been acting strange all day. Like a kid on Christmas Eve. On most Saturdays Nathan is usually exhausted from working all week and prefers movies and a takeaway dinner on the couch. I'm normally the one who has to talk him into having our friends over.

He shrugs and casts his gaze at the freshly mowed lawn he'd spent hours on this morning. 'We missed Rory and Alison's gatho two weeks ago so it's been a while since we all caught up. I'm just excited to see everyone.' He slips an arm around my waist and draws me closer. 'And the boys are at your mum and dad's, which means we get to sleep late tomorrow,' he says, planting a kiss on my forehead. 'We need this, Loz. You need this. You've been so stressed since you've gone back to work. You need to take it easy and have some fun.'

He's got a point. I have been feeling highly strung lately. But it's so hard to switch off from work at night and switch back on to being a mum. I don't have as much energy to help the boys with their homework anymore, and I miss my afterschool chats with Leni. And apart from a quick wave from the front lawn, I hardly get to catch up with my friends anymore.

He raises his beer and I tap my wine glass against it.

'To a good night,' says Nathan, holding my gaze over his beer.

'To a great night,' I say, my husband's optimism rubbing off on me.

'That's my girl,' says Nathan grinning.

Birds twitter and flit between branches of the shrubs in our front garden. It's a lovely autumn evening. Still warm, despite the cooler nights we've been having.

I raise my glass and take a huge gulp of wine, and allow the delicious sauvignon blanc to wash away any lingering niggles of dread.

* * *

Hours later, the wine has definitely done its job and I'm feeling pretty good.

That is, until my husband opens his mouth and shares a secret that wasn't his to tell.

'Hey, Laura, tell everyone what your mum told you last week. You know, about the...' Nathan, his face flushed from too many drinks, pauses to take a sip of beer from his frosty stubbie and waggles his eyebrows at me '...the *sex* parties.'

Though I remain composed in front of our guests, inwardly, I'm annoyed. He knows this is a vault subject. Something that I specifically asked him to never share. Of course, when I bring this incident up tomorrow morning, he'll likely blame the alcohol.

'Your mum? Sex parties?' says Orlando, his eyes glazed from too much booze. He collapses into a chair next to his wife, Samantha, the alcohol giving his lean and wiry frame some added weight, and groans. 'Can she get any hotter?'

I roll my eyes at Orlando and cast a sympathetic gaze at Samantha. Usually Sam has a good-natured laugh at her husband when he speaks about his milf crush on my mum. But tonight, her expression could be carved out of stone, and it's not a happy one.

'Oooh, what's this about sex parties?' asks Alison, who is standing at the entrance to the games room, pool cue resting against her palm, her dead-straight blonde hair spilling over her faux-tanned shoulders. Her voice oozes sex, just like her pouty lips and curvaceous body. Right now, I'm pretty sure most of the guys in the vicinity are thinking about how they'd kill to be Rory, Alison's husband, for just one night.

Our games room opens up to the dining room, where most of our guests, all neighbours from our little dead-end street, are gathered around our large wooden table which right now is covered with bottles and glasses – some almost empty, some half-filled with alcohol, and what few crumbs remain of my cheese and cracker board.

Michael, the only single man on our street, who's just finished a game of pool with Alison, enters the dining room with raised brows and hands his victor a cold beer before he sits down next to Rory and gives him a friendly slap on the back.

Rory gazes across the room at his wife, Alison, the expression on his face that of a kicked dog. She's been avoiding him all night and I wonder what's up this time. I can never quite work those two out. They're one of those couples where you wonder how they fit together. Outwardly, yes, both are tall, blonde and stunning to look at. But inwardly, they are like two magnetic poles being squeezed together, resulting in repulsion again and again.

Not that Nathan and I are perfect. He annoys the heck out of me sometimes. Like just now. And I'm sure I annoy him just as much in other ways. But we are opposite poles that just can't help but attract. Migrating back to each other's arms no matter what. Nathan jokingly calls me his bestie with benefits. He says he's lucky to have his best mate and lover all wrapped up in one. I agree with him.

Alison leans towards me, her freshly cracked beer foaming out of the spout, and murmurs seductively, 'Do tell.' Her perfume clouds my head and I lean back slightly.

'More importantly, Laura,' says Orlando, throwing me a lazy, alcohol-afflicted wink and attempting to steeple his hands together, 'did your mum actually *participate* in these sex parties?'

'Oi, quiet, you,' I say, shaking my head before popping the last crumbling cube of vintage cheddar into my mouth. I'll have to go on an extra big walk tomorrow to burn off all the cheese I've been eating tonight.

Samantha elbows Orlando in the ribs – she's had some rum from the bottle Michael brought over. Rum has always made Samantha moody and extra sensitive. My brother has always been the same with rum. Me? I get emotional on vodka, so I stay away from it. Nobody needs to see me bawling my eyes out and telling everyone how much I *really, really* love them.

Anyway, Orlando is so intoxicated he barely notices Samantha's irritation and continues to stare up at me from his seat, his dark eyes glazed over.

'Come on, we need *details*, Loz,' he says, slurring his words.

I make a this-is-awkward face at Nathan, and he mimics me then shrugs as if to say, we've opened the vault now, no use shutting it back up.

I sigh before gulping down a mouthful of shiraz. I'm on the red now. Not the smartest move, mixing my drinks, but the spicy alcohol warms me and I must admit, I'm feeling pretty good, much better than I'd been feeling earlier today.

Nathan was right. I really needed this. It's so nice to have everyone over at our house again.

'Hurry up with the sex party stuff already,' says Alison, snapping me out of my thoughts.

'Okay, okay, so…' I clear my throat and immediately adopt David Attenborough's style of speaking. 'Many years ago, people… humans… partook in what was known as key parties. The males would toss their keys into a fruit bowl and the females would then each select a key, resulting in the selection of their mate for the night.'

'Oh, you mean a swinger party?' asks Naomi, her deep brown eyes thoughtful and her raven hair glossy beneath the dining room light.

'Yep.' I nod, grimacing. 'My parents were invited to a party once and didn't realise it was for swingers.' A giggle tickles my throat as I picture the scene. 'Mum walked into the house carrying a plate of ham and pickle sandwiches and the first person who took one was a naked man wearing an Alf mask.'

'What's an Alf?' asks Alison.

'A hairy alien from Melmac,' says Samantha impatiently, rolling her eyes at Michael who suppresses a laugh. Samantha and Michael went to primary school and high school together, giving them the kind of bond and in-jokes that can only come from sharing your growing years.

'Gosh, that mask would be worth heaps nowadays,' says Orlando, shaking his head, the thought sobering him momentarily.

Usually, Rory gives Orlando a good ribbing about his obsession with collecting unusual objects and keeping them until they're 'worth a million one day', but tonight he remains quiet, his face straight as he puts the beer to his lips.

'Oh my God, so your milf mum was a *swinger?*' says Ollie, slapping his hands on the table, the monetary worth of the Alf mask forgotten. 'I am... officially... blown away.'

'Can you shut up, please, and let Laura tell the story?' says Samantha, before knocking back the rest of her rum on ice, then signally with a nod for Michael to pour her another.

Michael glances quickly at Orlando, who's too busy staring into space, probably picturing a younger version of my mum tossing a plate of sandwiches aside and ripping her clothes off.

Perhaps sensing the growing tension between Samantha and her husband, Michael only pours her a small one and navigates it around a couple of empty glasses, a half-eaten cracker and a red wine ring until it slides into her waiting hand.

'Cheers,' she says, before knocking it back, draining the glass. But Orlando doesn't even notice.

By now, every pair of eyes in the room is fixed upon me. It's a strange thing, holding court like this. I'm unaccustomed to this kind of attention. It's Nathan that loves to regale an audience with captivating stories.

'Did they stay and have sex?' asks Naomi, learning forward, clearly getting into the conversation.

'And did your mum get rooted by the Alf dude or what?' asks Orlando.

I take another gulp of wine and silently apologise to my mother who made me promise not to share. But I tell myself that it's the same as Mum telling everyone the story of when I was ten years old and sleepwalked into Mum and Dad's bedroom and did a wee in their wardrobe, right on top of Mum's 'brand-spanking-new!' pair of suede, knee-high boots.

'Mum never said. All she said was that they stayed for the party.'

'They *stayed*,' says Nathan, his brows raised.

Alison finishes off her beer with extra gusto and slams it on the table.

'They totally had sex. She just doesn't want to gross you out.'

'Maybe,' I say, shrugging, not really wanting to think about it. My wine glass slides around in my sweaty palm – having all eyes on me has made me nervous despite the booze giving me a spot of courage. 'But the interesting thing is that they were all neighbours like us. Can you believe it?'

'Wow,' says Naomi, eyes wide and thoughtful. She takes a long sip of her wine.

Samantha looks beyond disgusted as she glares at everyone in the room.

I clear my throat. Time for a change of subject. I can literally feel the eyes of the men sizing up us women in the room. And I don't like the way Alison is smirking at Rory, who is eying the floor with a morose expression on his face.

'Okay,' I say, blushing when I catch Orlando staring at me for longer than I'm comfortable with. 'That's the end of the story. Let's talk about something else now.'

A brief silence descends upon the room before Orlando slaps his hands against the table. 'Imagine if we all did it... had a party like that one.' He grins at everyone in the room, avoiding the watchful gaze of his wife.

Samantha gets up and kicks her chair back so hard that it hits the wall and chips a thin shard of the off-white paint from our dining room wall.

'Sam,' I call after her, raising my brows at Nathan, who shrugs in return.

'It's only a bit of fun, Sam,' he calls after her. 'We're just mucking around.' He gives his friend a playful shove. 'Orlando's not serious, are you, Ollie?'

'I frickin am,' says Orlando. 'I wanna do it.'

To my absolute surprise, there are a couple of murmurs of agreement in the room, followed by nervous giggles.

Samantha bursts back into the room, a prominent vein running down the centre of her forehead, her cheeks flushed.

'Okay, so, when do we do this thing?' she says and shrugs. 'Look, I'm in as long as Michael puts his keys in the bowl.' She folds her arms across her chest and smiles with evil intent at her husband. It's no secret that Orlando resents Samantha and Michael's close friendship.

Michael drops his rum and Coke, which fizzes all over the shag rug beneath the dining table.

'Sorry,' he mutters beneath his breath, glancing up at me sheepishly, as though I'm in charge of the carpets in the house, when in fact Nathan is the one who vacuums most of the time. He likes making neat, even lines of freshly fluffed carpet fibres. Lines which the kids do their best to flatten out almost immediately after their father has created them.

'Don't anybody get too excited,' I say, forcing a laugh. 'It's just an old story. It's not like any of us would actually do it.'

Nathan grabs a tea towel from the rack in the kitchen and kneels down to blot at the wet patch on the rug.

'Would you do it, Naomi?' asks Michael, wiping his dripping hands on the tablecloth, his face serious.

The room falls silent and the air is suddenly thick with sexual tension. It's no secret that Michael has had a little crush on Naomi in her recently widowed years.

Naomi takes a sip of her white wine, her dark eyes thoughtful, and sighs.

'I'm not sure.' She shrugs her shoulders gracefully and throws an almost apologetic glance at me. 'Maybe? I mean, I miss it… I miss being touched.' She blushes a deep pink beneath her dark skin and shakes her head. 'But then again… maybe not. I mean, it would be so weird because we all know each other.'

No one says anything by way of reply. It's been a lonely five years for Naomi since her husband, David, passed away, and nobody would dare judge her.

'What about you, Rory? Would *you* do it?' asks Nathan.

Rory raises his blond head, but before he opens his mouth to speak, Alison, her blue eyes icy, snorts a bitter laugh.

'If any of you women here are prepared to be disappointed, go for it.' Alison twists open a fresh beer, her long, acrylic nails glittering like jewels beneath the dim dining room light. She tosses the twist-top at the table. It lands in the cashew nut and basil dip. 'As for me, I'm up for it. I'm up for some adequate intimacy.'

*Ouch.*

Nathan and Orlando grimace at the same time. I throw a sympathetic glance at Rory.

'Wow,' Michael mutters from the end of the table. He gives Rory a supportive pat on the back.

'I'm going to ring Mum and check on the kids,' Rory says, getting up from the table, his long fringe, sun-bleached from years of surfing, covering his eyes, his back and shoulders rigid.

'Far out, Rory, can you leave them alone for one second? You're home with them all bloody day. Give it a rest already. Let them have fun with their grandparents,' says Alison, her face red, her teeth bared in undisguised disgust.

But Rory is already heading down the hallway, glowing phone in hand.

I feel so bad for him, and judging by the new uneasy vibe in the room, almost everyone else does too. Except for Alison, who happily rests her pool cue against the wall and reaches for a rice cracker and the last bit of brie.

Alison has never been my favourite person in the street. It's not that I don't like her… we've just never been close. I'm not sure she's close to anyone, to be honest. She's got a great big invisible wall wrapped around her and I've never managed to break through it to get to know the real Alison. But, after that low blow to Rory, I'm not sure that I even want to.

Rory is such a great guy, always doing favours for his neighbours despite having his hands full being a full-time stay-at-home dad. I've always had a soft spot for him. He's definitely the sweetheart of the street. Most of the women in the neighbourhood and nearly all the mums at school have a bit of a crush on him. It doesn't hurt that he looks a bit like Brad Pitt from his *Legends of the Fall* days. What surprises me the most is that Rory's sweetness is lost on his own wife.

Alison does have a stressful job, though, and I understand, now that I've returned to work, just how hard it is to be a working mum. But still. No need to embarrass your partner like that in front of the entire street.

'What about you, Laura? Would *you* do it? Would you screw someone else other than Nathan?' asks Alison, licking her full lips. 'He's your only one, isn't he?' she says, eyeing Nathan. 'So, you've never experienced a different dick.'

Some of the guys choke on their mouthfuls of beer. Michael sets his freshly poured rum and Coke down and proceeds to have a coughing fit. Nathan reaches over and thumps Michael on the back until the coughing subsides.

'Cheers, buddy,' says Michael, blinking away the tears that have formed in his almond-shaped eyes.

'Jesus,' says Orlando, widening his eyes and then grinning at Samantha, forgetting for a moment that his wife is severely annoyed at him. He looks at me, brows raised in disbelief. 'Old Nate's your only one? We've got to change that, surely.'

I take a swig of my wine, draining the glass, my eyes zeroing in on my husband.

I met Nathan when I was nineteen and married him at twenty-one, much to the bemusement and in some cases, plain hostility, of some of our friends and relatives. Yes, Nathan has been my only one, but I'm glad because he is the only one for me. There has never been anyone else. Sure, I've fantasised about others sometimes – actors mainly, sometimes random, almost faceless men, but that's just harmless fantasy stuff. Things I'd never do in real life. I still enjoy sex with my husband. I love him. We've got a good, solid marriage.

'So?' presses Alison. 'Would you?'

Seven pairs of eyes watch me. I glance at Nathan and smile. But when I open my mouth to say, 'no,' that Nathan and I are happy and we don't need to have sex with other people, Nathan opens his big fat mouth and cuts me off.

'Well, *I* wouldn't say no, that's for sure,' he says waggling his ginger eyebrows at everyone in the room.

My heart sinks and I can't speak, but I manage to force a smile in front of everyone.

'Well, well, well. Laura,' says Orlando, a big grin on his lips. 'Pick my keys please, because if I squint my eyes, I can see your mum.'

'Are you for real, Ollie?' says Samantha, shaking her head.

I sigh and set my glass down and throw Nathan a death stare.

'So, who needs another drink?' asks Nathan, getting up and heading over to the fridge. The way that he drums his fingers against the open fridge door and sings along to the music playing in the background, as though he didn't just admit that he'd sleep with another woman, hurts like hell.

'Not for me.' Naomi stands and pushes her chair in. 'I'm picking the kids up from David's parents early tomorrow. Matthew has a soccer game.'

'Noooooo,' I say. I wanted to have a good one-on-one chat with Naomi, as we haven't had much of a chance lately since I've returned to work.

'Sorry,' says Naomi, coming to plant a kiss on my cheek.

'I'll walk you home, if you like,' says Rory, who has reappeared, phone in hand, a frown on his face.

'Where are you going?' snaps Alison.

'I need to get an early one,' says Rory. 'I was up until three last night. Dylan couldn't sleep.'

Alison rolls her eyes. 'Yeah, well, you get to sleep during the day while the kids nap, so, you can't be that tired.'

Rory's cheeks tinge red and his body stiffens again.

'Thanks, Rory,' says Naomi. 'But I'll be fine to get home myself if you want to stay longer.'

'Nah, I'm leaving anyway.' His blue eyes lock with mine, and I swear he's speaking to me telepathically, saying, *yes, our partners are arseholes, aren't they?* But out loud he says, 'Thanks for the drinks, guys. Catch up soon.'

'Pop over anytime you need a chat,' I say, hand over heart.

'Yeah, mate, anytime,' says Nathan.

I hold the door open, inviting the warm, early autumn air and the scent of frangipanis from my front garden into my house.

'Sure thing,' Rory says, stepping out into the night behind Naomi.

'Bye,' says Naomi, throwing me a sympathetic glance. 'I'm sure everyone is just mucking around.'

By 'everyone', I know she means Nathan.

'Me too,' I say, smiling. But deep down I'm not so sure.

# 2

## *Naomi*

Naomi turns on the hallway light and stands at the front door, waving at Rory who awaits her signal in the driveway.

He waves back and she watches him leave, the streetlights illuminating his blond ponytail against his dark blue shirt, until he disappears into the darkness.

Naomi had refused his gentlemanly offer to come inside and make sure there wasn't an axe murderer waiting for her in the shadows. But now as she closes and locks the door behind her, the sound echoing off the hallway walls, she wishes she'd accepted it.

A yawn escapes her lips, her body's exhaustion helping to take the edge off her fears of being home alone as she does a quick check of all the rooms in the house.

It's late and she wants to prepare for next week's online therapy sessions by going over her clients' notes tomorrow after Matthew's game. Plus, she'd promised the kids she'd take them to the park in the afternoon, but they might have to settle for an afternoon of watching movies. But she suspects they won't mind if she throws a bowl of hot buttery popcorn into the deal.

Naomi shivers, her skin prickling at the silence and emptiness of her home.

Being alone is the worst. She hates it and can't wait to go to sleep, wake up and drive to her in-laws' house and collect the kids. But she does it because she knows the kids and David's parents need precious time together, and she knows that it's healthy for her to go out and have a drink with other adults.

But the house is just not a home without the vitality and lightness of the kids. They have a way of brightening up the gloom.

Still yawning, she boils the kettle and makes herself a chamomile tea in one of her grandmother's chipped old cups, and takes it with her into her bedroom where she undresses and gratefully slips into her comfy pyjamas, still stained with the hot chocolate that her youngest boy, Riley, had spilled the night before.

She smiles at the memory, grabs a novel she's been trying to finish for weeks from her bedside table, and sits up against the bedhead with her pillow stuffed behind her lower back.

But after finishing her tea and reading over the same page mindlessly, she decides to call it a night. Not just because of Matthew's early soccer game and the notes she needs to prepare, but because she is so used to waking up with her early-bird children that early mornings have become an ingrained habit. There is no David to gently kiss her at dawn and suggest she lie in while he takes care of the kids for the morning. Just herself.

Her eyelids are so heavy. However, once her head hits the pillow, she cannot get the conversation at Laura and Nathan's house out of her head.

The way everyone had looked at her when she'd said 'maybe'. She knows they talk about her sometimes, and that some of them assume that because she is now single that she should date Michael, the only other single person on their street, and re-join the happy-couple gang she and her husband had once been a part of. They mean well. She understands they are only trying to help her and that they worry about her loneliness.

But she's not lonely for just any man.

It's David she misses.

David that she wants.

She misses him so much that she physically aches for him. She misses the feeling of his strong arms around her. She misses his laugh, the sound of his voice, his smell. Everything.

And yes, she could most certainly do with some intimacy, to be touched and to touch a man again, but she doesn't want to sleep with any of her neighbours. Even Rory who is so lovely.

She wants David and only David in her arms.

Naomi sighs and rests a hand on her husband's pillow and caresses it as though caressing David's cheek.

Tears form and spill down her face to soak into the pillowcase.

Life just isn't the same anymore.

She never asked for it to be like this. For endless nights alone in a cold bed.

Naomi wants to be with David and the kids, laughing in the yard, having fun sharing the task of cooking a barbeque while slowly working through a nice bottle of chilled white, watching the kids play and be silly.

She wants it so bad she aches inside to think that no matter what she does in life, no matter how hard she works, no matter how much she tries to be a good mum and a good person, she will *never* have that life again.

# 3

## *Tristan*

Tristan watches Leni dash across the street and, minutes later, smiles as she waves at him from her bedroom window, which is situated directly across from his. She is still dressed in his hoodie, but her long blonde hair is now twisted up into a knot on top of her head.

Both having bedrooms on the second floor of their homes on opposite sides of the street has allowed for much entertainment over the years.

He waves back at her before throwing himself onto his bed and reaching for the phone on his bedside table.

Leni is already messaging him, those three dots sending his heart rate spiking.

> Leni: *Tonight was so great :-)*
> Tristan: *Thanks. Did you really enjoy it?*
> Leni: *Yeah, like... a lot :-)*

He thinks about how carried away they'd gotten. How warm and soft she'd felt in his arms. How her body fit so perfectly against his. And her kisses, *oh God*... He groans and rolls onto his back.

Everything about her, her laugh, her smile, her touch, her voice... he just loves everything about Leni and wants so desperately to be with her right now. No amount of time spent with her is enough. She's like a drug he's become addicted to. A good one. The only side effect being permanent horniness, and, according to his mum, extreme dopiness.

He'd wanted to climb through her window later tonight, and spend the night by her side, but she'd said no because her parents would be cleaning up after the party and would still be awake.

Tristan sighs. He'll have to make do with his thoughts – all of them about Leni, of course. He smiles to himself as he pictures her, the girl he's known for most of his life.

They hadn't always been like this – an actual couple. They'd been best friends since kindergarten, and for years he'd thought of her as only a friend, until about three months ago when they'd gone to the beach together.

They'd been messing about, throwing each other around in the choppy sea and bodysurfing until their bodies ached and their fingers were numb prunes. They'd crashed together on the shore and had rolled around on the cool wet sand and wrestled with each other. He'd pinned her down, and as she squirmed beneath him, he had grown hard. He'll never forget the look on her face when she stopped laughing because she'd felt him, felt *it.* At first, he'd been mortified and had started apologising for his wayward body, but she'd blushed and tugged on his wet hair and dragged him in for a kiss. To say he'd felt surprised would be a total understatement.

He closes his eyes and relives their first kiss inside his mind. She'd tasted like salt and... heaven.

From that moment on Tristan ceased to think of Leni as the kid across the street he'd known all his life. She had become beautiful Leni, the girl he is madly in love with. It was as though the friendship veil was lifted and they could see each other for who they truly are – two souls meant for each other.

Tristan is crazy about Leni, knows everything about her, faults and all, and loves her more than anything or anyone he's ever loved in his seventeen years of life. Even more than his parents. And he loves them so much.

He and Leni have already professed their love for each other, and have made plans to get married and have children later on, after travelling the world of course.

They've been an official couple for over three months and have agreed on everything except when they'll have sex.

Leni wants to wait. She said she's only sixteen and feels nervous about it. Tristan wants to do it now. He wanted to do it tonight. He wanted to do it yesterday, last month, last year, a lifetime ago. At least that's how it feels sometimes.

But he loves her. He has promised he'll be patient and so he will. There is no other girl he wants anyway. He'll wait forever if he has to.

He yawns and starts tapping at his phone.

'I love you,' he texts.

'I love you too,' she writes back immediately.

As his lids grow heavy, and his warm phone rests against his beating heart, Tristan falls asleep thinking about just how perfect and wonderful life is when you love somebody.

And how even more wonderful it is when they love you back.

# 4

## *Orlando*

'Did you have to bang on about Laura's mum so much? It was funny in the beginning, but now it's plain creepy,' says Samantha, putting her phone on silent before slapping it against the bedside table.

She yanks on the blanket hard, so that most of it lands on her side of the bed, then rolls over to face the bedroom window.

Moonlight streams in through a gap in the curtains, illuminating a thin strip of Sam's cheek. It is enough for Orlando to see that his wife is tense. Angry. Furious even.

'And it's humiliating for me. Like, you fantasise about an old wrinkly woman in her sixties as opposed to your own bloody wife. You never talk about me the way you talk about Laura's mum.'

Orlando gently tugs on the doona until he is able to cover at least one leg and arm.

'Oh, come on, love. It was just a joke. I had too many drinks and I thought it was funny.' He sighs, knowing he'll have to be careful or Sam will give him the cold shoulder all night, if not for the rest of the weekend.

He cautiously shuffles closer to her warm body.

'Sweetheart, I'm the luckiest man in the universe and I don't need to tell everyone on our street about it, because they already know.' He spoons her and she allows it. A good sign. He slides an arm around her waist. 'I bet everybody who meets us thinks, my God, how did that ugly bastard get *her,* that goddess? And do you know how they'd answer that thought?'

She giggles, her body jiggling in his arms.

He leans in so that his lips graze her earlobe.

'They'd think, he must have a huge–'

'Ego!' Samantha jiggles in his arms some more.

'Oi.' He laughs. 'You know what I've got is way bigger than my ego. And that's saying something.'

She bursts out laughing and he takes that as his moment to give her a little tickle so that eventually she turns and puts a hand to his cheek and smiles.

'Okay, you're forgiven, you absolute dork.'

Relief courses through Orlando's veins. He hates making Samantha mad. Hates that he made her feel so insecure tonight. He's an idiot when drunk. Booze makes him reveal every stupid fleeting thought in his brain. Most of the time he just tries to get a laugh out of everyone. But tonight, he knows he went too far.

They kiss. It's a brief one. But Sam is smiling when she pulls away.

Orlando reaches out and strokes his wife's auburn hair.

She smiles and rolls back over to face the window. 'Night, love.'

He wants more, but the kiss is enough for tonight.

'Goodnight, my darling.'

*Happy wife, happy life.*

It's bloody true, thinks Orlando.

# 5

## *Rory*

Rory enters his silent home and heads straight for the fridge. Once he has a beer in his hand, he goes out the back door and stands in the garden beneath the moonlight.

As he stares up at the simple beauty of the starlit sky, he wonders where it all went wrong. Where and when his happy life turned unhappy.

He wonders if he's any different to Naomi.

In a way, he feels as though he has been widowed. That he lost the old Alison he married. The woman whose eyes used to light up at the sight of him. The woman who used to smile and laugh. The woman who used to love him.

Now he feels as though he's living with a stranger who looks like Alison. And no matter what he does, there is no pleasing this strange woman.

He's tried to talk to her, tried to help her through whatever it is that happened to her before she met him, the secret thing that she refuses to share.

Once, Laura mentioned how after childbirth, women can become undone. That whatever they bury from their past can rise up like bile and poison their lives with bitterness.

Rory wonders about that. He's always known that Alison has a lot of skeletons in her closet, things about her past that she won't speak about – like her relationship with her father. And he's respected that.

But now... now he wonders if he should have maybe done more about it. Helped her process it all before the kids came into the picture.

He feels responsible somehow. Especially now that Alison's behaviour is starting to affect the kids.

Just like with Rory, she's beginning to push them away.

Rory blinks away the sting in his eyes and forces the beer down his throat, past the hard lump that threatens to unravel him.

Tomorrow is another day, he thinks, and spills the rest of his beer on the lawn.

He showers and then climbs into a cold bed and tries his best to fall asleep.

But instead, a million ideas poke at his brain, and after an hour of restlessness, he gets up and goes into the kitchen, puts the kettle on and makes himself a steaming mug of coffee. The strong earthy scent of the rich brew invigorates him.

He takes the pale green notepad and black pen his wife keeps by the phone, and sits at the dining room table, moonlight streaming in through the kitchen window the only light.

Rory isn't sure if this will work. He isn't quite sure if his wife cares enough to read what he writes. But he must try. He must reach her before she is truly lost to him.

*Dear Alison,*
*I have a confession...*

# 6

***Laura***

I stare at the ceiling while my husband snores softly beside me.

Since I've known Nathan, I've always admired his ability to sleep soundly after spending hours with friends, with all that alcohol and coffee circulating in his system.

Right now, I'm so wired. On nights like this my brain has no off-switch. I get like this whenever I've had people in my home. The gatherings never fail to provide me with lots of food for thought and I always feel as though my friends have left something of themselves in my home after they've been. Ghosts of their energies lingering in the atmosphere, messing up the vibe of my family.

I'll burn candles in the morning, and switch on my diffuser. Mandarin and lavender oils are such an uplifting scent first thing.

I smile in the darkness as I picture Leni upstairs in her bedroom, likely messaging Tristan. He's such a lovely boy and already like a son to me and Nathan. We've known him since we moved into the street and Leni started kindergarten, and after the years have passed, the transition from daughter's friend to daughter's boyfriend has been an easy one.

The only downside is that they are so young and I worry about them. You go through so many changes at that age and it's never guaranteed that both will harbour the same feelings for each other in a year or so. It'd be a shame to lose their lifelong friendship over a bad breakup.

But for now, I'm happy to watch Leni blossom and grow into a young woman in love. Her smile, whenever Tristan is around, is so precious it melts my heart.

Nathan's snoring gets louder and more guttural so I nudge his arm.

'Roll onto you side,' I whisper.

He makes a choking sound for a second, then clears his throat and rolls over. Soon his breathing settles into a more peaceful rhythm.

I sigh, enjoying the peace, and allow my thoughts to drift over some of the conversations from tonight. My mind zeroes in on the key party discussion.

Was Nathan serious? Could he actually sleep with one of our friends and then continue on as normal?

I shiver and sink beneath my doona.

Though I'm certain it will all be laughed off in the morning and Nathan will shake his head and say, 'no way, Loz, it's just you and me', I can't shake the way his eyes had lit up at the idea and the easy way he'd admitted that he 'wouldn't say no'.

There's no way I'd sleep with any of our neighbours. Or with any man for that matter, no matter who. Sure, I've occasionally checked Rory out and wondered what kind of lover he is, but that's about as far as it goes. Fantasy and reality are two completely different things.

The more I think about it, the more unsure I feel about Nathan.

Does our sex life satisfy him? Is he looking for more?

Up until now I would never have questioned our sex life, but since learning that Nathan 'wouldn't say no', I'm not so sure anymore. Maybe our three-nights-a-week routine bores him. Maybe our love life is too predictable.

The ceiling creaks as Leni moves about on the floor above us.

My imagination takes flight. I picture my daughter returning home one evening to find Nathan having sex with Alison on the dining room table, only to flee upstairs to discover me and Rory going at it against the stair rail. I shudder at the thought.

While Nathan continues to sleep soundly beside me, I work myself into a state of panic, creating a whole imaginary disaster. One where we need to move out of the street and relocate because of the aftermath my imagined key party inflicts upon us all. Marriages destroyed, our children's lives never to be the same again.

I should never have mentioned what Mum had told me in confidence.

But I've done it now.

For several minutes, I try deep breathing to help calm myself. It helps somewhat. But my mind keeps straying back to the key party conversation.

Surely though, after waking up tomorrow, everybody is going to be more worried about curing their hangovers than a silly conversation everyone likely won't remember.

* * *

The delicious scent of coffee brewing and bacon frying wakes me in the morning. That, and the sound of Nathan and the boys chatting downstairs.

After a lazy stretch I get up, unable to remember the last time I'd slept late.

I recall being unable to get to sleep last night, still staring up at the ceiling when the dawn birds began to sing. I must have fallen asleep just as the sun came up. No wonder I've slept in.

'Morning.'

'Morning, Mum, you lazy sleeper-inner!' says Billy, our youngest, beaming his cheekiest smile.

I ruffle his messy golden curls, then the darker curls of my eldest boy, Austin, my heart full, and sit down while Nathan places a fully loaded breakfast plate in front of me, followed by a steaming mug of coffee.

'I was going to bake a cake and bring it to Mum and Dad when I picked the boys up,' I say, wondering why they are already home.

'Your mum called and said your dad's hearing aid is on the blink and he wanted to go in and get it looked at before the hearing centre closed at lunch. So, I got the kids early.'

'Oh, okay. Where's Leni?'

'She's probably sexting Tristan,' says Austin, nibbling thoughtfully on a piece of toast.

I widen my eyes at Nathan, who swallows down a laugh with a mouthful of coffee.

'Mum, can we please play on the Xbox?' asks Billy, leaning into me and staring up at me with his gorgeously huge, deep brown eyes. He has such beautiful lashes. Leni had ranted and raved once, about the unfairness of both boys having such lush, long, dark lashes while hers are spare and blonde.

'I don't know... Sunday is a day for chores, not Xbox.'

'But you had a party last night,' says Billy. 'Today is our turn. Me and Austin can have an Xbox party.'

Austin, busy shovelling in the last bit of his scrambled eggs, pleads with his sparkling, hazel eyes, his brows raised in hope.

'Please, Mum?'

'Oh, go on then, enjoy your Xbox party.' I grin at them both. 'I'll join you two later,' I say, winking. 'And if you're lucky, I might just break out some of those cool Fortnite moves I've been practicing.' I mime a dance in my seat.

'Um, please don't,' says Austin, already out of his seat and carrying his plate to the sink. 'Nobody does that anymore. It's really not cool.'

Billy has crammed an entire half of toast into his tiny mouth, so he can't speak, but his little shoulders and his light brown curls shake with giggles as he carefully carries his plate to the sink, dropping a bacon rind in his wake.

I watch them, warm pleasure in my heart as they bounce off, their bare feet slapping against the tiles until they disappear into the games room like bats to a cave.

'What's all this about?' I say, smiling. 'I normally only get brekky on Mother's Day.'

Nathan leans over and presses his lips to my cheek, his stubbly chin prickling against my skin, before sitting back down. He smells fresh and clean and his hair is still damp from a shower.

'Hey, there's nothing I wouldn't do for my beautiful wife.'

I hover between wondering what I've done in life to deserve such an amazing husband and questioning why he is doing this.

Nathan opens the newspaper while I chew on a grilled mushroom that he so lovingly prepared for me. Am I a bad wife for suspecting there is an ulterior motive behind this breakfast?

'I've been thinking about what we discussed last night,' he says, winking at me from over the sports pages.

*Bingo.*

I take forever to swallow down a forkful of scrambled eggs, and wash it down with a sip of coffee and a feeling of dread.

Uneasiness churns my stomach. The breakfast had been such a surprise that I nearly forgot about my hangover. My head begins to throb.

'What do you mean?'

He rolls his eyes. 'About the key party,' he says in a low voice so the kids won't hear. Not that they can. I can hear them shrieking and laughing from the games room.

I set my coffee down and my abandoned fork clinks against the plate.

'Oh.'

So, the breakfast and the waiting on me is not an apology for what he said last night, it's so that he can have sex with one of our neighbours. Lovely.

I wonder which one. Samantha? Naomi? Alison? I'm not exactly sure why, but Nathan sleeping with Alison would bother me the most.

'Yeah,' he says, his eyes bright with enthusiasm. 'I'm thinking life's short so why not do it?' He reaches across and puts his hand over mine, as though this is a loving moment to be savoured. 'What do you think, love? Just the once? Just to... I don't know... experience it. It might spice up our sex life.'

My skin crawls at his touch.

'What's wrong with our sex life? Seriously. I bet nobody in the street does it as much as us.'

'Three times a week is hardly a lot.'

'Last week we did it five times. *Five* times.'

He shrugs.

I draw my hand away.

'It's not like I'm unsatisfied,' he says. 'It's just... I just want to see. To see what it's like... with another person.'

A shiver travels down my body. All of a sudden, I'm in desperate need of a shower.

I stare down at the mountain of food in front of me and stand.

'Thanks for going to all this trouble, but I might just skip breakfast and get a quick shower.'

Nathan falls back into his chair and rolls his eyes like a child.

In the bathroom, as I strip off my clothes, I wonder at the heart's ability to love someone so intensely, even when they disappoint you and irritate the hell out of you.

Steam fills the bathroom after I turn the shower on full blast and super-hot, but I get the feeling that no amount of soap and scalding water can wash away this feeling of dread that clings to my skin.

# 7

***Leni***

Leni wakes up with a smile on her face. She's had a dream about Tristan. A good one. They'd been together, just holding hands and staring in each other's eyes, sitting on the greenest grass she'd ever seen, the kind only found in fantasy, with the most glorious sunshine beaming down upon them, warming their skin.

Her lower belly still flutters from the effects of staring into Tristan's deep green eyes, the windowpanes of his beautiful soul, even if it had only been a dream.

The first thing she does after she opens her eyes is reach for her phone, checking to see if he has written.

Of course, he hasn't. He loves to sleep in. She smiles to herself as she pictures him snug beneath his doona, his brown hair messy, his dark lashes resting against his cheeks.

She sends him a text anyway.

*Good morning, cutie.*
*I had a dream…*
*About us.*
*I'll tell you all about it when you wake up*
*So, wake up, please :-)*

After going through her social media feeds, which don't really offer anything as exciting as Tristan anymore, she decides to take a shower. Last night, Tristan asked her to come over in the afternoon and she intends to be ready for anything.

Humming a tune and thinking only of Tristan, Leni strips naked, poses a couple of times in the bathroom mirror, admiring and criticizing herself at the same time. She imagines Tristan watching her, wonders what he'll think of her naked body when he eventually sees it, then turns the shower on and steps beneath the hot gushing water.

Her heart beats a little faster as she wonders if she is ready to take the next step in their relationship. Tristan has made subtle hints, little movements and gestures which suggests he wants to touch her a little more intimately and wants her to reciprocate the favour. And while the idea of touching him gives Leni a thrill, she isn't sure that she is quite ready for actual sex, or if she even wants to do it yet.

As Leni rinses conditioner out of her hair, she makes a mental note to google some how-to sex stuff before she heads over to Tristan's house, and to maybe even watch a couple of those embarrassing videos on that porn site everyone is always talking about at school. She wants to be as prepared as possible so that she doesn't look a complete noob. Especially since Tristan has had girlfriends in the past, so is way more experienced than Leni.

She turns off the shower, dries herself and puts on an oversized T-shirt. Despite it being April already, and autumn, the days are still warm. The weather can still pass for summer.

With her hair damp and smelling like strawberries and cream, she throws herself down onto the bed, opens her laptop and gets stuck into her research.

She wants to surprise Tristan. Give him an afternoon to remember.

And though the very idea of doing anything beyond kissing and holding hands makes her blush so hard she feels as though her cheeks are about to melt off, she is going to make sure she at least gives it her best go.

# 8

### *Alison*

A quiet rage builds inside of Alison as she reads the letter Rory had written for her last night. He must have done it after he'd gotten home, while she was still at Laura and Nathan's house. But she hadn't seen it until now.

She hadn't seen much at all by the end of the night. She'd barely made it to bed in one piece she'd been that drunk. There'll be a large bruise on her thigh where she bumped into the credenza in the living room when she was trying to find the bathroom in the early hours of the morning.

While Rory is still sleeping, she reads and reads his words over and over. She pictures him sitting in the moonlight, emotion dripping from his heart onto the paper as he writes.

It's enough to make her stomach turn.

*I have a confession...*

For some reason, those words are what anger her the most.

When she first started reading it, she almost thought he was actually confessing to something horrible he'd done. Something evil. Something she could then use to justify her abhorrent behaviour towards him.

But no.

It was far from that.

His words have only served to make her feel worse.

More despicable.

More despised.

More hated by her own self.

She screws up the paper into a ball and stomps out the front door to the recycling bin, where she promptly throws it in amongst the aluminium cans and cereal boxes.

Let them mash his words up into a pulp along with the other trash.

Alison leans against the brick mailbox and watches the morning birds as they flitter between branches. They are beautiful with their gorgeous colours. Rainbow lorikeets. But she feels disconnected from them. From their beauty, from their song. From the nature all around her. The trees, the soft blue sky, the oncoming dark clouds low in the distance. Nothing touches her deep inside.

People at work go on and on about sunsets and sunrises and she nods and agrees with them, pretends to take pleasure in the wonders of nature. But the truth is she doesn't. She's not like other people.

It's as though when she was created, God forgot to connect a few wires or he left out some screws.

She's incomplete.

Nobody will ever understand her.

Not even her own husband, whom, despite everything, she still loves.

How can she not? He's beautiful, kind, sweet and takes all the crap she gives. And somehow, *he* still loves *her*.

But it's his love that is the problem. His love that she doesn't deserve.

And to ensure that his love doesn't have a chance to find its way to her undeserving heart, she is doing the only thing she knows, and if she does it enough, then maybe, just maybe, he will finally stop loving her and she can go about her life being who she really is.

Her dad will have been right.

And then everything will be as it should.

# 9

## *Michael*

Michael slams the tray of his utility shut and secures the latches before hopping into the driver's seat.

He's just finished mowing his aunt's lawn, something he has been doing every fortnight since he was eighteen years of age. He began doing it after his uncle passed away of a sudden heart attack. It was not long after Michael's parents had moved back to Vietnam, where his father was born.

Back then, over thirty years ago, Michael had refused to accept the money his aunt had kept trying to stuff into his pocket or slip into his hands, and instead had gladly agreed to sit down to a delicious roast with all the trimmings and a slice of apple pie after the mow. The bonus was they both got to have a nice catch-up and his aunt had a bit of company for a change, a bit of chatter echoing through her large, immaculately clean, but empty house.

Truth be told, Michael needs the company. He's been on his own for so many years now that it is starting to get to him. It doesn't help that the one girl he has carried a candle for is married. He wouldn't exactly say 'happily' married, but she is still married nonetheless.

When Michael and Samantha had been in high school together, they'd dated for a few months and although they'd broken up, they'd continued to hang out and even used to say that they'd get married when they got older. Michael had waited while Samantha had backpacked around Europe. He'd waited while she jetted off to live in Bali for six months in her twenties, attempting to find herself and learn the art of mindfulness and meditation. He'd been patient.

But then, on her last week in Bali she'd met Orlando, who is an okay guy apart from being the main obstacle to Michael's life plan and lifelong dream.

In truth though, Michael can't find it in himself to hate the guy.

After he'd, purely by chance, moved into their street, a quiet cul-de-sac, he quite liked catching up with them and the rest of his neighbours on a fortnightly basis or the odd front lawn chat. He never has to worry about drinking and driving because all of his mates are right here on the street.

The bonus being that he gets to see Samantha all the time now. And though she is well and truly taken, with a son and all, he values their friendship above all else, so he is pretty happy in that sense.

Still, he is human. He wants someone special to share his life with, he can't deny it. He thinks about it all the time.

And now there is this talk of having a swinger party. He'd practically fallen off his chair the other night when Samantha had said she'd gladly participate. Even quiet, thoughtful Naomi had seemed interested. Just hearing her say 'maybe' in that low sexy voice of hers had excited him. It got him wondering what she would be like in the bedroom. With those dark, secretive eyes and her quiet, mysterious demeanour, he imagines that she is a tigress in bed.

He wonders if he should listen to the others' advice and ask her out. Samantha and Orlando are always at him to step it up and pursue Naomi. But he's always been mindful of the fact that Naomi still seems as in love with her husband as she had been when he was alive. There is a sadness in her dark eyes, and Michael has always felt like he'd be intruding on an existing relationship if he asked Naomi out. It feels wrong somehow.

But that 'maybe'... perhaps she *is* finally ready to move on. Or it could be that the loneliness might be getting to her too. Or maybe she only wants the sex. Which is completely fine by Michael. He could help her out there. For sure.

But the more he thinks about it, while he watches his footy team lose on the telly, the more he realises that he doesn't want just sex. He wants the cuddles, the long breakfasts together. He wants to share his bed with a warm body every night. He wants the joy of shopping for someone on their birthday and special occasions. He wants to make somebody feel special.

Yeah, he thinks, nodding his head.

Forget the swinger party. He is going to go over to Naomi's during the week and ask if she'd like to come over for dinner. She can bring the little ones too. He is pretty good with kids. He'll buy them treats, but maybe healthy treats in case Naomi is one of those mums who doesn't like their kids to eat any sugar.

Nah, she'll be chill, he thinks, draining the last beer dregs out of his stubbie.

He casts his gaze around his house, at the blandness of it, and decides that one beer is enough. If he wants to entertain a sophisticated woman like Naomi, then he'll have to scrub the place up a bit. Starting right this minute. He brushes a hand across his grizzly chin. And maybe he could do with a bit of a spruce-up himself.

# 10

### *Naomi*

Naomi opens her eyes and tries to make sense of the sound.

She's in bed, encased in the warmth of her duvet, her brain deliciously foggy and fresh out of a dream about David. They'd been talking. About what, Naomi can't remember. But she is smiling and the tingling warmth of just being in the presence of her husband lingers.

The squeak of brakes and the dull roar of an engine clears the fog and sets her heart pounding.

Bin day.

*It's Monday already?*

Naomi sits up and can see that her bed is littered with the notes she'd spent hours working on late last night. She'd stayed up until 3am and now it's past six and she's forgotten to put the bins out.

But at least she's prepared for the fifteen online appointments booked in this week. Her clients' mental and emotional wellbeing are more important to Naomi than the weekly rubbish collection.

Still, she gets up, races out the back door and up the side gate, her bare feet slapping against the cool pavers. The dawn birds are calling to each other and the sky is a soft, baby blue tinged with apricot.

Grabbing both bins, one handle in each hand, she runs across the damp lawn, dragging them onto the driveway and up to the street verge.

The recycling truck is at Rory and Alison's and Naomi pauses and catches her breath as she watches it upend their bin into the truck. A ball of paper tumbles to the ground and bounces off the curb, rolling in Naomi's direction. It lands in front of Michael's house.

It's then that she sees Michael carrying his lunch bag and coffee flask, about to get into his ute for work.

He waves and she waves back, crossing her arms over her chest when she realises that she ran out into the street in her sheer silk nighty.

'Naomi! Wait!' he calls after her as she begins to dash back inside.

She inwardly curses and turns around, her arms wrapped around her chest.

'Oh, sorry,' he says, blushing when he reaches her driveway. 'I didn't realise you were...' His words trail off and he turns his head to watch the recycling truck collect his rubbish.

'I slept in,' she offers, by way of explanation.

'Oh. I would have put yours out if I'd have noticed them missing. You were too quick for me.'

Naomi smiles and she can see that Michael still can't meet her eyes and his face is still flushed. He's nervous. She senses a question coming.

'Um, Naomi,' he says, finally meeting her gaze. 'Would you and the kids like to come for dinner one night this week?'

Naomi feels trapped. Michael is so kind to offer to put out her bins if she ever forgets, and now he has offered to make her dinner. And the kids.

She feels obliged to say yes.

But she doesn't want to.

She likes Michael, but she can tell that he likes her more. And that is dangerous to Naomi. Because if she doesn't reciprocate his feelings, even after a nice dinner, she's worried that she will have given him the wrong idea and he will get hurt.

The recycling truck pulls up and they both take several steps back and laugh as the noise of the machinery puts an end to their conversation momentarily.

Once it moves on, Naomi has gathered enough confidence to reply to Michael's dinner invitation.

'Oh, thanks for the kind offer, Michael. But I'm swamped with clients this week. And the sessions really exhaust me by the end of the day, unfortunately. I get so tired and cranky.'

Michael puts both palms up in mock surrender. He looks relieved that it's over.

'We can't have you getting cranky,' he says, grinning.

Naomi laughs. Michael is a sweetheart, she thinks.

'Well, I'm going to be late for work. You take care, Naomi.'

'You too.'

Naomi feels relieved that there's no awkwardness between them and watches and waves as he drives away to work.

A tiny breeze picks up and tickles her bare skin while she stands there watching the quiet street in the early morning light.

That ball of paper from Rory and Alison's recycling bin rolls down the street and hits her bare ankle.

She picks it up, pulls it open, and smooths out the paper.

It's a letter.

A letter to Alison.

From Rory.

She knows she should just pop it in her now-empty recycling bin and be done with it.

But her heart is beating wickedly fast.

It's a thrilling feeling.

She has Rory's heart in her hands and she can examine it any time she likes.

Naomi heads down her driveway, her pulse throbbing in her ears.

She wonders why Rory's words have set her brain and body on fire like this, without having even read them.

The kids are starting to stir and call for her when she returns to the house and she quickly enters her bedroom and without reading the letter, tucks it in her bedside drawer.

She doesn't know when she'll read it.

It's wrong. It's an invasion of privacy.

But she knows that she will do it anyway.

# 11

*Two weeks later*

***Rory***

Rory steps under the warm shower to wash off the salt from his morning swim. The conditions hadn't been good enough for a surf, but simply diving into the cool ocean had helped him to clear his head and put him in a better headspace for tonight.

He isn't ready for another get-together at Laura and Nathan's, as much as he enjoys his neighbours' company and as much as he'd like to celebrate Nathan's birthday with him.

But spending another night in Alison's company, along with their friends, is not something he's looking forward to. He can put money on the fact that his wife will find something to insult him about in front of everyone. She's been extra hostile this week. Distracted too. He's tried multiple times to reach out to her, to ask what's wrong. But the more he questions her mood, the moodier she becomes and the greater the distance between them grows.

But Alison has just returned from dropping the kids off at her parents' house for a sleepover, so the evening with friends is happening whether he likes it or not.

Rory would have much preferred they use the opportunity of being kid-free to perhaps order in some takeaway, share a bottle of wine and respectfully discuss the emotional distance in their relationship – the lack of laughs, the lack of affection, the lack of intimacy. Rory can't remember the last time he'd had sex with his wife. It's been at least a year. He has to rely on taking care of himself each day in the shower. That is about as much affection and intimacy as he receives these days – and it's from his own hand.

Not that he is a demanding husband. He has never treated sex as though it's his right or anything like that. But he needs *something.* And it doesn't even have to be sexual. A soft touch. A gentle smile. A kind word or two. Something to prove that he is still loved.

It hurts. It hurts that each day, when his wife returns home from work, she looks at him like he's ruined her day. Like Rory simply existing is the cause of her sour mood. Just like that, the humming, grinning woman who enters the front door and hugs her children vanishes and glares at him, silently accusing him of being there.

Rory steps out of the shower and after drying off and getting dressed, he enters the living room, where his wife sits hunched over a notepad, pen in hand, scribbling some kind of a list.

He's about to crack a joke and ask if she's maybe writing him a love letter, but thinks better of it when she glances up at him and offers a smile. Sarcasm and pettiness will only make things worse. And strangely enough, that smile, although slightly ambiguous, encourages him to approach things a little differently.

As he passes her on the way to the fridge, he leans down, thinking to press his lips affectionately against her blonde head while she writes.

'Jesus, get away, I've only spent an hour doing my hair,' she says, darting her head away from him, leaving behind a waft of perfume.

Rory straightens and swears beneath his breath. He enters the kitchen and gets a beer out of the fridge.

When he closes the door and spies the picture of him and his three kids from a teddy bears' picnic the local council had put on for mums and dads and their kids, tears come to his eyes. He wishes they were here now. When he's with the kids he feels the closest to complete.

He swears to himself again. The last thing he needs is for Alison to see him cry. She'll likely call him a pussy or a wuss and tell him to man up.

He presses the palms of his hands into his eye sockets, hard, rough, and mentally tells himself to harden the fuck up, and walks through the kitchen and out the door to the garage.

The electric door groans and rattles as it opens, and Rory makes a note to take a look at it Monday morning.

The lawn feels crisp beneath his feet and the setting sun has turned the whole street golden.

Naomi calls out to him, a huge smile on her face, and waves from three houses down the street. She's wrangling her kids into the car, backpacks in tow.

'See you later on,' she shouts before getting into the car.

Rory's heart stirs. Naomi. He feels for her loss and hates seeing her without David, even after five years have passed. David was such a good bloke. Rory misses him.

Rory sighs and takes a sip of his beer.

'Oh, I wondered where you'd gotten to. What do you reckon?'

Alison holds out a piece of paper and waves it at him until he comes over and takes it.

'What's this?' he asks, for one foolish second thinking it an olive branch.

'Read it and find out.'

She folds her arms across her ample chest, as though ready for confrontation.

Rory shakes his head at what she's written. It is not what he expected, to say the least.

*Key Party Rules.*

Rory locks eyes with his wife and raises his brows.

'What the hell is this, Alison?'

'It's rules for tonight. For Nathan's birthday.' She shrugs. 'I reckon we give Nathan his birthday wish.'

Rory shakes his head again.

'I'm pretty sure he was just mucking around. There's no way Nathan would actually do this, and it didn't seem like Laura was too interested in the idea anyway.'

Alison rolls her eyes.

'Well, you're wrong. She's changed her mind. She wants her husband to have a perfect birthday.'

Rory laughs. 'Sure, sure.' He can still remember the way Laura's face had dropped when Nathan said he 'wouldn't say no' to a key party.

In fact, he can't imagine that anybody in the street would actually agree to this. Especially not his wife. He feels like laughing out loud at the idea of Alison wanting to participate. The woman who hates sex and has rejected every single advance of his in the past year. It just doesn't make sense. He doesn't understand what she's trying to achieve.

For a moment, though, he wonders if the night will work in his favour. Would seeing Rory disappear into a room with another woman make Alison jealous? It's a possibility. And it's not like he'd actually ever sleep with anyone else. He'll just play along and see how far he could take it before she realises that he is still a desirable man. That's if this ridiculous idea actually happens.

'Well, I'll believe it when I see it tonight,' he says, shrugging. 'But I suppose it reads okay. No spelling errors if that's what you're worried about.'

Alison grins.

'Why are you grinning like that?'

'Are you worried your wife will finally get some satisfaction?' she asks, a smirk on her pouty lips.

Rory studies his wife's face. For someone so beautiful on the outside, he can't believe how rotten she can be.

'That's a laugh coming from you.' He takes a pull of his beer. 'I pity the poor bastard you get. He's in for a long wait.' Rory looks at his watch-less wrist. 'He might get some action in about a year's time.'

Rory doesn't expect the shove against the wall, the rough bite of the brickwork digging into his back. His wife is a tall woman, only an inch or two shorter than him and he's six foot four. She dwarfs all the women in the street. And though she doesn't scare him, he's shocked by the physical assault. Shocked that she wants to hurt him. As if the emotional abuse isn't enough.

After half a minute of highly charged silence between them, she backs away, her cheeks flushed, her eyes alight with something Rory doesn't recognise and never wishes to see again, before she disappears inside the house, slamming the door behind her.

Rory glances in the direction of Naomi's place and can see that Naomi has only just returned from dropping the kids off – probably to her in-laws who live only a couple of minutes away. She turns her head quickly, as soon as she sees him. Great, he thinks. She saw the shove, he's certain of it, and now she's probably embarrassed on his behalf.

The emasculation of Rory.

He hates that somebody has seen. Hates that he is now a man who has allowed his wife to push him around.

Shame floods his face with heated blood. He retreats into the garage so that nobody can see him, then drains his beer and gets another one. He only ever drinks when the kids are being babysat. He can go a fortnight without a drink. But tonight, tonight he feels like drinking himself into a stupor. He welcomes the distraction of Nathan's birthday celebrations.

Now he hopes that Alison is right. He hopes that this key party stuff isn't just some ridiculous conversation that they had all gotten a laugh out of. He hopes it *is* serious. Even if it is just going into a room and having a conversation with another woman – someone who will listen to him without judgment. Because that is exactly what he needs. Only, he hopes that he doesn't get Naomi. Because there is no way he is going to be able to look her in the eye and feel like a man after she's seen him get pushed around by his wife. She must be repulsed by him.

But then again, he's not fussed who he gets, really, he'd rather be with anyone else than his wife right now. He isn't even sure he wants to be with her at all anymore, full stop.

However, as swiftly as that thought arrived, his mind drifts back to the times when they cared about each other, back to when they were two young people in love sharing their lives together, making plans, experiencing everything new and wonderful about being a couple of soulmates.

He cannot believe that he's let it slide for so long. That they've *both* let their relationship become what it is now. Something defunct and not a relationship at all.

Now his blood warms with anger, not shame.

The night can't come any sooner for Rory.

He needs to let off steam. To have a drink. To blank out his problems for just one night.

To hell with Alison. He is going to stay as far away as possible from her tonight.

Then maybe he will have an okay time.

# 12

## *Tristan*

Tristan opens the front door to his home and lets Leni in, along with a warm evening breeze that stirs fallen brown leaves around in the driveway.

Across the road, Leni's house is all lit up and he can see movement through the window where the curtains have been left open. He wonders if he and Leni will settle down in a street like this when they are older, a place where everybody supports one another like family.

Leni smiles shyly when she enters, her cheeks tinted pink, bringing with her the scent of berry shampoo and the mango body cream she always uses. He can't wait to hold her in his arms. He wants to do it right now, but he reminds himself to go easy. The last thing he wants to do is smother her with over-eager affection.

He studies Leni's face, and when their eyes meet, she quickly shifts her gaze to her feet.

She's nervous.

And that makes him nervous.

'How are you?' he asks, his voice coming out cracked and wrong.

She smiles and meets his gaze for one second before looking away again.

'I'm good, thanks.'

Pleasantries.

Tristan feels strange. Sad almost.

After twelve years of being practically conjoined twins they are now acting like strangers. He hopes he hasn't caused this new distance between them from coming on too strong. From wanting too much from her.

'Have you had anything to eat? I could make us something. Toasted sandwich or... two-minute noodles?'

'Um, yeah I'll have a toastie. Thanks.' She grins and grabs his hand and gives it a squeeze. 'I'll help.'

With great relief, Tristan smiles, and feels the tension in his shoulders melting. His heart relaxes to a steadier beat. Okay, so maybe things aren't as bad as he thinks. Maybe he's overthinking everything, like he always does.

In the kitchen, working together feels normal and Tristan is grateful for the small reprieve from obsessing about how things will go tonight.

They laugh when they bump into each other a couple of times, and she slips her arms around his waist easily while he tries and fails to keep all the orange juice he is pouring in the drinking glasses.

But later, after they finish eating and drinking, and put their plates in the sink, the air around them thickens with awkward tension again.

Sex. Why did he have to want it so badly? Why couldn't he just forget about it for a while. Stop thinking about it until she tells him that she's ready.

Even just being alone in the house with Leni makes Tristan's hands shake, his voice crack. The slightest touch or even just the smell of her hair sends him dizzy. Just the idea of going upstairs into the bedroom with her tonight is enough to keep him in a permanent state of excitedness.

If he's honest with himself, he wants it over with – that's how nervous the idea of sex with Leni is making him. It's the post-coital cuddle, where they get to hold each other after having done it, that he's looking forward to. Then they can just relax and do it without the nerves in the future.

He watches Leni help herself to a glass of water, the tumbler trembling in her grip, and he feels bad for her. He wants to sweep her up into his arms and reassure her that everything is going to be okay, that sex isn't a scary thing and that he will be gentle, but she looks so skittish right now he doesn't want to overwhelm her or scare her away.

When she's finished her water and placed the glass in the sink, slowly, as though avoiding the fact that they are alone in the house together, he offers his hand.

'Do you feel like watching a movie in the theatre room? Or do you want to go up to the bedroom?' he asks, wanting to give her the option of the movie in case she isn't ready. 'We can just veg out on the couch if you like.'

She remains silent for a while, then releases a gentle sigh which sounds like relief, as she takes his hand.

'Let's watch a movie first. If that's okay with you.'

He gently tugs her into his arms and kisses her cheek.

'Of course, I'm okay with it. I'm happy when you're happy.'

She grins, seems to relax and the two of them choose a movie and settle on the couch.

Tristan starts to wonder if it will happen at all, but, as he watches Leni's face relax and feels her body melt against him as she snuggles in close, he knows that he will wait forever if he has to.

Because Leni is the one for him.

# 13

## *Laura*

I shiver as the cool air of the refrigerator tickles my bare shoulders. I pass the cold meat platter I'd prepared earlier to Nathan for him to place on the dining room table, then shut the fridge door with my hip and shiver again as I collect the cheeseboard from the marble kitchen benchtop. But this time I'm not shivering because of the cold, I'm shivering because I'm freaking out.

Everybody is either sitting or standing around the dining room table, empty shot glasses in front of them, while Alison holds court reading aloud a list of rules she's crafted for 'the street's very first key party'.

Inwardly I shudder. This had better be a stupid prank Alison is playing on Nathan, because there is just no way that we are holding a key party tonight. It's a simple gathering for Nathan's birthday. A few drinks, some nice cheese and a couple of laughs. That's all.

The worst part of this is watching my husband gaze at Alison as though she's some kind of God. The usual, happy, family man Nathan would be cracking jokes by now about how ridiculous this is. But no, his green eyes are riveted on Alison in the most serious way and it gives me the chills.

Even if Alison says 'gotcha!' after she reads her so-called rules, the cold truth is that Nathan wants this. He wants the opportunity to sleep with other women. And it kills me to know that. I'm not even sure that I can put it behind me and just forget this after tonight either. Even if nothing happens. How can I forget his eagerness to sleep with another woman other than me, his wife? How do I stop my mind from overanalysing his interactions with my female friends from now on? How do I get used to this strange world where my iron-strong sense of trust has been compromised?

I've always been secretly chuffed that we've garnered the 'Romeo and Juliet' tag within the group, the token star-crossed lovers. It's always been a bit of a flex. Not in a showy way. Maybe pride is the correct word to describe how I've always felt about our solid marriage. Pride that I'm now having to swallow down like something jagged because it is obvious to everyone, from the awkward glances I've been getting, that my husband is no star-crossed, devoted Romeo.

Why did I have to go and ruin things a couple of weeks ago by mentioning Mum's stupid swinger party from the seventies? *The bloody seventies have a lot to answer for,* I think, shaking my head before popping a dried apricot into my mouth.

I slide a couple of bottles of good Margaret River red aside as well as the now empty bottle of vodka, and set the cheeseboard down onto the table before picking up my forgotten glass of sauvignon blanc. I swallow a large mouthful of the tangy, now-warm wine – I'm going to need it.

Alison clears her throat and I take my time, folding my arms across my chest, wine glass dangling between my fingers, before I look up and give her my attention. It's almost laughable the way everybody is staring up at her. Like she's Moses about to spout the ten commandments.

'Thanks for finally joining us, Laura,' says Alison, glaring at me before running her tongue over her top lip and giving all the guys a bit of a cheeky wink.

I raise my glass in mock salute but nobody is watching me. They're all watching Alison.

Looking at her right now, at all of her blondeness, it makes me wonder if Nathan has ever fantasised about her. Probably. With those long legs and those boobs and those eyes and lips and face... I sigh and drain my glass.

'Okay, so,' says Alison with a little too much enthusiasm in her smile. Her blue eyes glitter across the room at Michael, who shifts uncomfortably beneath her gaze and instead fixes his eyes on Samantha who raises her brows at him and grins. 'Rules.'

Samantha and Orlando poke each other's sides, both giggling, as though this is the best thing to happen to them and their marriage, which is exactly what Nathan had suggested about their own a fortnight ago at breakfast.

I wonder if it's just the vodka doing its job, loosening everyone up. Or maybe everyone here is a little more open-minded than me. Maybe I'm a closed-minded prude. But closed-minded or not, I can't help but feel as though I've walked into a parallel universe, a place where my own beliefs and feelings don't align with anybody else's.

'Rule number 1. Let's keep things traditional. All males will place their keys inside the bowl, after which each female, eyes closed, will select a set. If she chooses her partner's keys, she must place them back in and choose again.

'Rule number 2. Each couple must disappear together somewhere in the house, somewhere private. What happens in the room is up to the newly formed couple. They can have actual sex, or engage in other sexual activities, just make out, talk, or whatever they like. There are no rules as to what you can or cannot do together, as long as there is consent, of course.

'Rule number 3. What happens in the room, stays in the room. No going home and discussing with your partner what you and your swinging partner engaged in. All encounters must remain private and are to be discussed only between the two individuals during the encounter.'

Alison glances around at the room. 'This is to prevent jealousy issues from cropping up. Agreed?'

There are murmurs of agreement around the room, nods of heads. I hope this is because everybody is relieved to hear they don't have to have sex but can simply talk if they wish to. I know I'm most certainly relieved. But when I glance at Nathan, for a show of solidarity, a meeting of the minds, I get his side-profile. He hasn't attempted to catch my eye this entire time.

'Rule number 4. No contacting your key party partner after the act. No clandestine meetings, no secret text messages, no phone calls. We don't want affairs. This is purely about sex, not about pursuing new relationships.'

My heart contracts inside my chest at the mention of sex. It feels as though my ribs are closing in, squeezing at my most vital of organs. This feels wrong. So very wrong. I want to kick everyone out of my house. I want Leni home. I want to pick the boys up from my in-laws' place and I want to cuddle with them on the couch, watching Disney movies with blankets on our laps.

'Here, Loz,' says Nathan, catching my eye and refilling my glass practically to the brim. It's the first time he's looked at me properly in over an hour.

Just when I begin to relax and warm beneath his attention, he gives me a loaded wink, which makes my stomach turn. Why is my husband acting like such a creep? How has he never shown this side of himself before?

I gulp down half of my wine in a single mouthful and pray Alison finishes up with this rubbish soon and then we can all just laugh it off as one big joke and continue chatting, and hanging out like usual.

I think of the birthday cake I'd so lovingly prepared for Nathan, late last night. I'd purposely stayed up after he went to bed so that I could keep it a secret. It's in our second fridge in the garage, which I've been careful to keep Nathan away from all day. The cake's a golf course, complete with mini-Nathan holding a mini-club on top.

'Last one. Rule number 5. The most important rule. Protection.'

Alison slides out of her chair, gets up and crosses the room to open a large plastic bag she'd brought with her when she'd arrived. From it she produces a large purple, ceramic bowl and, my eyes nearly pop out of my head, a jumbo-sized box of condoms.

'Ha,' I say, faking a laugh and slapping my thigh. 'You're so funny, Alison. Gosh, as if this is really happening. Like seriously, guys?'

Uneasy murmurs start to rumble around the table.

'But didn't you get the text, Loz?' asks Samantha, who is on her third wine already, after downing four shots, her eyes glazed and blinking.

'What text?'

'Come on, Loz, we all got Alison's text,' says Nathan.

'Well, I didn't,' I say, not hiding the outrage in my voice. 'What was in it?' I'm starting to sound hysterical but I don't care.

Samantha gets up and shows me her phone. She opens WhatsApp and shows me a group chat that I'm not a part of. I wonder if I was purposely left out of the group chat.

Alison's blue eyes skip away from mine when I glance at her.

'See?' says Nathan. 'Whoever shows up for it, is *up for it*. You showed up.'

I want to have it out with him. Ask him how on earth he didn't notice that I wasn't in the group chat. And why he didn't bring the group chat up for discussion between us privately. Because if I'd been included in a group chat that is titled 'Key Party' I'd sure as hell would have told him about it.

'But it's my bloody own house so of course I'm going to show up. How come I wasn't included in the group chat?' I ask Alison, my face heating up.

When Alison ignores my question and instead begins to hand out condoms, I turn to Nathan, feeling rather drunk now, and point a finger in his face.

'We have a teenage daughter if you've forgotten. She's impressionable. Imagine she found out that we were all swapping partners and... fucking each other in every room of our house. She's just across the street, Nathan. *Across the street.*'

I meet Orlando's gaze across the table.

'What do you think Tristan would say? If he found out? Do you want this for your son too? Do you think he should fuck around behind our Leni's back? Do you think it's good for their relationship too?'

Orlando's eyes hold mine, a pink blush growing beneath his olive skin.

'Laura, I understand exactly what you mean. But you heard Alison. We can all sit in the rooms and just chat if we feel like it. It might even end up like... a bit of therapy.' He shrugs. 'It's like we get a hall pass to just chat and get inside somebody else's head for a while. It might actually help us.' He pauses and glances around the room. 'It actually might do us all some good.'

Rory has remained quiet, drinking his beer, his jaw set, his eyes icy as they fix upon his wife Alison, whose curvy body is drawing all the looks from the other men in the room. Normally they wouldn't look at her so obviously, but now, with the possibility of sex with

Alison actually within reach, it seems all the gentlemanliness has been cast aside.

Rory looks on the outside how I feel on the inside right now, and when our eyes lock, his face softens in silent understanding.

'Come on, guys, keys in,' says Alison.

Nathan gets up, and to my horror, plucks his keys off a hook in the kitchen.

In a last-minute move of desperation, I put a hand on his wrist.

'Don't do it, Nate. Please. We don't need this. We're good.'

Nathan holds my gaze, his greenish hazel eyes burning with a fire inside of him that I've never before seen.

'If you love me, you won't do it,' I add, pleading with my eyes, well aware that I'm resorting to emotionally blackmailing my husband out of this.

Nathan's keys land in the bowl with a jangly clank.

Rooted to the floor, I watch, spellbound as Orlando's and Michael's keys land on top. My stomach swirls sickly and I feel hot and cold at the same time.

'It's just a bit of fun, Loz,' says Nathan, not even bothering to meet my eyes.

Tears sting my eyes and make the room swim. I blink them away but more come.

Grabbing a nearly full bottle of sauvignon blanc and my empty glass, I flee the room and head upstairs to Leni's bedroom, ignoring everybody's pleas and cries that it's only a bit of harmless fun.

# 14

### *Naomi*

'You're next, Naomi,' says Nathan cheerfully, despite his wife, Laura, having only moments ago fled upstairs in a state of distress.

Naomi had followed after her, and tried to speak to Laura through the locked door of Leni's bedroom, but Laura had begged Naomi to leave her alone for a few minutes and promised that she'd return once she'd calmed down.

'Come on, Naomi,' says Alison, jingling Michael's keys in her hand – keys she'd selected from the fruit bowl for herself. 'Your turn.'

Samantha holds Nathan's keys in her hand, who is all smiles about the matchup.

Now Naomi is in the peculiar circumstance of being watched by all remaining eyes in the dining room as she tentatively reaches forward, her trembling hand hovering over the bowl, ready to select a partner for the night.

She isn't exactly sold on the idea of the key party and worries how it will affect the dynamics of the group. But she reassures herself that, no matter who she chooses, she isn't going to be forced to do anything that she doesn't want to.

Truth be told, the only one in the room she feels remotely attracted to is Rory. Because he is kind and sweet and a gentleman always. Even now, when the men were asked to toss their keys into the bowl, Orlando had to practically wrestle the keys out of Rory's hand because of his obvious reluctance to participate.

Naomi sighs and sneaks a sideways glance his way. It helps that he is cute and has long floppy, blond surfer hair, and a gorgeous smile.

But he is married, she tells herself, shaking her head and silently cursing herself for even contemplating anything happening between them.

Anyway. A nice chat with one of the guys will do no serious harm.

Naomi closes her eyes and lowers her hand into the bowl, where only two sets of keys remain. Orlando's and Rory's. The remaining set will go to Laura.

The first bit of cool metal Naomi's fingers brush against, causes her to shiver. Fate, she thinks, and curls her fingers around a key loop.

Whoops and cheers fill her ears as she selects a set and opens her eyes to find Rory avoiding her gaze, and shifting his feet – clearly uncomfortable, while the other guys swat him on the back as though he's just won the lottery.

Samantha gives Naomi a quick, celebratory hug before lightly shoving her towards Rory. Alison, on the other hand, merely raises her brows and mutters 'good luck' beneath her breath before she leans in towards her mate for the night, Michael, and presses her breasts against his arm.

Michael shuffles his feet uneasily and avoids looking in Rory's direction. He glances quickly at Samantha and raises his brows in a 'help me' gesture, before he takes a long drag from his beer.

Naomi's cheeks warm as Rory finally unglues his eyes from the floor and glances up. They make brief eye contact. They've always been able to sit and chat with ease whenever they've all gotten together, and she wonders now if this night will ruin things for them.

But deep down, she also breathes a sigh of relief. Whereas Orlando has been so eager for the key party to happen from the get-go, Rory, looks to be the complete opposite. And, perhaps once they are alone, they can chat like always and laugh about how weird this all is.

Her lower belly flutters as she moves to stand beside Rory and their arms brush. She wonders if she possesses the confidence to ask him for a hug. It would be nice to feel a man's arms around her again. She misses her husband so much. Misses the intimacy. A hug would be pretty special. Especially with Rory.

'Shit, does this mean I miss out?' says Orlando, staring at his lonely keys with wide eyes and looking like the left-over kid at school that nobody ever chooses for their sports teams.

'No way,' says Alison, who is running her fingernails along Michael's forearm.

Michael looks beyond uncomfortable, sweat making his brow gleam beneath the low-hanging dining room light, especially with Rory watching Alison's every move.

'Look, Orlando,' continues Alison. 'Technically your keys are the only ones left, so you get Laura.' She eyes the stairs. 'Now go up and find her, Ollie. Go get her.'

Orlando stiffens and glances at Nathan, but Nathan seems nonplussed about his good friend being paired up with this wife and merely turns his head and leans forward to Samantha, whispering something in her ear that makes her giggle.

'Okay,' says Orlando, giving Samantha a long look. He opens his mouth, as if to protest, as if to say he wants out of this arrangement, but instead glances at the staircase and exhales, his shoulders drooping. 'I guess... I guess I'll go upstairs then.'

Naomi, unable to stand the tension in the dining area, takes Rory by the hand and leads him down the dimly lit hallway and into the laundry.

'Sorry, I just couldn't take it anymore. It's just so bloody awkward in there. Let's go sit outside.' She opens the linen cupboard and seizes a thick grey blanket before leading Rory out through the laundry's sliding door and into the backyard.

The air is sharp and chilled, and their breaths come out in little white puffs.

'How did it get so cold? It was so warm today,' says Rory, rubbing his hands together. 'Actually, it was warm up until about an hour ago.'

'I know,' says Naomi, sitting down on the loveseat. She stills the swing's motion with her legs until Rory sits down beside her.

He takes the blanket and spreads it over their laps as the seat begins to gently rock.

'Comfy?' he asks, a shy smile lighting up his blue eyes.

'Yep,' she says, her heart racing unnaturally fast. It's only Rory, she keeps telling herself. Sweet, neighbourly Rory. Great dad. Great friend. All round nice guy.

'So,' she says, shifting in her seat beneath the blanket and staring up at the house. Rory follows her gaze and they both sit in silence watching shadows move upstairs and downstairs. Naomi wonders how Rory must feel, knowing that his wife is inside the house somewhere, alone with Michael. At least Naomi doesn't have to go through that. Knowing that somebody else is with her sweet David. She fully understands Laura's reaction to this.

Rory, whose large feet are dragging against the ground, gently pushes against the pavers so that the swing continues to sway. He looks down at his beer and starts attacking the label with his fingertips, scratching off as much as possible.

Naomi feels her shoulders relax. Poor old Rory is a nervous wreck.

'Hey, look, we're swinging,' she says, giggling at her own joke.

Rory glances up and smiles, his blue eyes shining with delight.

It makes Naomi grow warm inside, to know that she is responsible for putting that joy on Rory's face and in his eyes. She has a sudden, innate desire to make him happy, which is not completely selfless – she also wants to know if she still possesses the ability to affect a man, if she still can summon up that magical womanly power which she thought may have died along with David.

'Okay, so, do you just want to chat?' he asks, rubbing his left hand up and down his blanket-covered thigh. He takes a sip of beer. 'Or we could, if you like, cuddle. But only if you want to. I mean, I'm up for a friendly hug if you are.' He exhales noisily and drops his head a little, his eyes now hidden by his long fringe.

Naomi feels her heart squeeze.

Her husband David had always liked Rory. They'd always migrated to each other at parties. So, Naomi is certain that if David is looking down at her this very minute, that out of all the men she could be intimate with, it would be Rory that David would be the most okay with.

'Okay. Yeah. That would be nice actually,' says Naomi, her voice cracking at the thought of her long-departed husband, but her heart pounding in anticipation at the prospect of feeling the arms of a man around her again.

They both raise the blanket at the same time and laugh softly into the cool night air. Naomi hesitates briefly before sliding towards Rory.

He welcomes her, opening his arms and wrapping them around her. She can't help but feel stiff and awkward at first, but then finally releases a sigh and relaxes against him, allowing herself to melt into his warm embrace. She rests her head against his shoulder, and they both breathe out in unison and share another giggle.

It feels weird at first, but only for a few seconds, then it suddenly becomes strangely natural to be sitting here burrowed against Rory's chest. She allows her forehead to sink into the place between his shoulder and neck. Lovely. She trembles a little, but not from the cold. She feels perfectly warm against his body.

Rory, too, begins to relax – she can feel it.

He exhales again, softly this time, his breath a silvery mist, and relaxes into her.

Naomi breathes in deep and quietly sighs at the scent of his skin – fresh and clean, with perfectly balanced hints of soap and man. She instantly regrets soaking her own neck in her too-strong perfume. If Rory were to kiss her there – not that she is intending for it to happen of course – she would taste bitter. David used to complain about it and would love to pounce on her, fresh out of the shower, so that he could taste her bare, 'un-poisoned' skin.

After David died, Naomi had been reluctant to wear perfume. Though she knew it was ridiculous, and pointless, keeping her skin perfume-free just how David had loved it, had made her feel somehow connected to her dead husband.

However, in this moment, five years on, she finds the idea pitiful, and can clearly see herself now, as a woman who has failed to move on, who has clung to the death of her husband as though 'widow' is her identity.

She shivers and feels her eyes sting. Why does hugging Rory make her *feel* so much? There are so many emotions swimming around inside of her right now, she isn't quite sure what exactly she's feeling. Sadness? Anger? Fear? Self-disgust?

Rory clears his throat and finds her hand and gives it a squeeze.

'I miss David too,' he says, and the softness in his voice makes Naomi want to sob, to really bawl.

Rory must sense her rising emotions, because he draws back a little to meet her gaze. She quickly averts her eyes and straightens her back, gazing up at the stars before she speaks.

'It's okay. I'm glad somebody has the guts to speak about him. Everybody acts as though his name is forbidden or as though I'm going to burst into tears at the mere mention of his name.' Naomi meets Rory's gaze again. 'You know?'

Rory smiles. 'Well… I *can* see tears forming in your eyes.'

Naomi smiles at Rory's attempt to lighten the moment.

'Yeah. But they're happy tears – most of the time.' Naomi exhales. 'I just want everyone to acknowledge that he's still a part of my life, my children's lives. I don't want him put away. Not yet… at least I think I don't.'

'Yeah, I totally get that. We should all talk about him more. Talk about old times.' He smiles at her. 'I'd really like to do that. You can pop around after work anytime you want to chat about him. I'm home with the kids, usually just cooking dinner.'

'What about Alison's rules about not seeing each other alone after this, after tonight?'

Rory blows air between his lips. 'Stuff her rules. Why should she get to make them all? We can make a couple of our own. Plus, you can bring your kids over and they can play with mine. So, we won't technically be on our own.' He smiles, then stares down at his beer.

A long, but peaceful and easy silence passes between them.

'I'm glad I got you,' says Naomi, squeezing his hand. 'I honestly probably would have just made excuses and left if I'd gotten one of the other guys. They just all seem so...'

'Sex-starved?'

Naomi laughs, the two white wines she'd quickly shared with Laura before everybody else had arrived, and then later, the vodka shots, are still working their way through her veins, making her feel warm and cosy.

'Exactly,' says Naomi. 'They behave as though they haven't had sex for years.'

Rory shifts a little in his seat and meets her gaze, his cheeks turning pink beneath the dim outdoor light.

'Well, I hate to break it to you. But I'm probably the only man here who comes under that category. Not years. But... a year is about right.' He seems embarrassed by the reveal and glances away, staring off into the darkness where Laura grows her vegetables in a long, rectangular patch.

'Really? I thought Alison, with all her... sexiness, that she'd be... I don't know, sex-mad or something.'

Rory laughs softly and drops his head back against the cushion of the swing.

'No. That's all a mask she wears. She's not sexy at all. She's angry most of the time. It's like, she likes the looks, the attention, the compliments, but that's as far as it goes. She has no interest in sex at all.'

Naomi makes a silent 'oh' with her lips.

'That's... well, that's pretty sad.' She leans back against the seat and turns slightly to face Rory. 'I saw you two, this morning,' she says, thinking back to what she'd seen – Alison shoving Rory. 'You two were arguing. Are things always that bad?'

Rory's jaw twitches and his eyes turn shiny.

Naomi hopes he isn't going to cry.

When he doesn't speak, she glances up at the house and decides to change the subject.

'Gosh, I wonder what they're all doing in there? Surely, they won't use the kids' rooms. That would cross the line for me. I don't know how everyone agreed to this, in all honesty.'

'True,' says Rory, who seems to have relaxed again now that the subject is not his marriage. 'You could tell poor Laura wasn't happy about it. She was never into it.'

'Yeah. It's all Nathan, let's be real.'

'Yeah.'

Rory takes another sip of beer and then puts his empty bottle on the ground beside the swing, the clink echoing into the quiet night.

'So how do you feel about it all? This idea of swinging,' he asks, his voice low and his gaze curious.

Naomi stares into those expansive blue eyes of his, at his handsome face, at his lips, and thinks to herself, if Rory was single, she would ask for a kiss, but he's not. *He. Is. Married.*

'I don't know,' she says, shrugging, her heart racing. 'I guess... I don't really know.'

Rory nods and sighs. He swears beneath his breath.

'Are you okay?' Naomi asks.

'Yeah.' He shakes his head. 'I'm that much of a fool, you know. My wife's probably up there fucking Michael and I'm sitting here, too scared to put my arms around you again.'

'I thought you said she didn't like sex?'

Rory sighs. 'Yeah, sex with *me*. Maybe she'll like it with someone else.'

Naomi feels her heart twitch.

'Well, *I* could hug *you*. How about that? That way I'm the bad guy.'

Rory swallows thickly, then nods. 'Yeah. I'd like that.'

Naomi opens her arms and he leans into her, sliding his own arms around her waist and resting his face in the crook of her neck and in her hair. She feels his warm breath against her skin and relishes the sensation.

Tears form in her eyes, but she blinks them away and starts to rock slightly, as though Rory is a child she is soothing, or perhaps they are both soothing each other. She closes her eyes and listens to his breath become slower, and feels his heart beat in time against hers.

Bliss, she thinks. This is bliss. This is what she has missed. Oh God, and how she has missed it. She thinks of David. She tries to measure this hug against the ones she'd shared with her husband but she finds she can't quite recall the feeling, and this devastates her.

Blinking away fresh tears, she moves her hands up and down Rory's back and lightly runs her fingers through his long hair until she realises that he's fallen asleep. She smiles to herself, relaxes back against the seat and closes her eyes, allowing herself to truly *feel* the magic of this moment.

She must have fallen asleep herself because all of a sudden, she hears somebody crying and tries to sit up, but feels the weight of Rory in her arms. At that moment he jolts upright, rubbing at his eyes.

'We must have fallen asleep,' she says, blinking.

'Who's crying?' asks Rory, rubbing his face.

Naomi glances around at the dimly lit yard and fixes her eyes on Laura, who stands several meters away beside the laundry door, wiping at her eyes.

'Laura?'

'Is that Naomi?'

'Yeah. And Rory,' Naomi says.

When Naomi gets closer, she can see that Laura's face is flushed and stained with tears.

'Are you okay?' Naomi feels so stupid asking that, because of course Laura is not okay.

'No. I'm not. This was a terrible thing. I should never have let this happen. I should never have allowed this under my roof. In my family home.'

Rory takes Laura into his arms and she begins to sob again. He offers no words of comfort, but simply rubs her back, making soothing shushing noises.

Naomi watches, her heart melting, as Rory soothes their friend as easily as though he were soothing one of his own children.

'I don't want to sleep with Orlando. I just want everyone to go home,' Laura says between sobs. 'I hate this. I hate it.'

Rory watches Naomi over Laura's shoulder and extends a hand to her. She takes it and gives it a squeeze as she stares into his eyes.

Over Laura's sobs and mutterings, all Naomi can think about is that she is so glad that she'd gotten Rory as her partner for the night. Her bare arms are still tingling from his touch.

But she is also glad that they'd only hugged. Because even though Naomi and Alison aren't the closest of friends, and despite the fact that Alison was the head campaigner for the key party, nobody deserves that kind of betrayal.

Naomi thinks of the letter she has tucked away in her bedside drawer. The private words of Rory's that she's forbidden herself to read.

She knows she'll be reading them tonight.

# 15

### *Leni*

Leni stares up at the ceiling as she replays over and over again, what she and Tristan had done only an hour ago. Not much in the whole scheme of things, that is, compared to what a lot of the other girls at school have been doing with guys since they were thirteen. But to Leni it is so much.

Heat rises to her face as she recalls how it had felt to touch him. The thrill of it.

But no matter how wonderful it had been, she had still felt the need to stop, asking Tristan if they could just hug instead in the end. She isn't sure that she is ready to go further just yet. She isn't actually sure when she'll be ready and it frightens her because she knows how eager Tristan is to have sex. And although he tells her again and again that he'll wait forever if he has to, she knows this can't be true. Not according to everything she's ever read or watched or heard about boys.

Even though they hadn't managed to go all the way tonight, they'd clung to each other for ages afterwards. Even now, it still takes her breath away to think about it. She's never felt such powerful emotions for anybody before. Has never loved someone so much. And it isn't just the silly kind of crushes her friends at school have on guys they hardly know. This is the real deal. She has known Tristan for almost all of her life.

A tear rolls down her cheek, and she rolls onto her side, where the pillowcase absorbs the wetness from her face.

Leni's heart starts to work itself into a panic as she stares at the tiny patch of starlit sky that she can see through her bedroom window, blinking through the branches of the gigantic tree that grows in the front garden of her house.

She feels like this sometimes. Frightened. Whenever things are going well in her life. As though something dark is going to swoop down and ruin it all. She's had these kinds of feelings since she was a small child.

Once, when she was only about five or six years old, she was watching the sun cast its morning rays over her father's flower bed through her bedroom window and she remembers thinking how wonderful and fun and perfect life was with her mum and dad and two baby brothers. But no sooner had her little mind thought this, a dark cloud had shifted over the sun, draping the flower bed in grey shadows. She can still vividly recall how sad she'd felt in that moment, how morose, how bleak.

She had known how fragile life was, even at that age, how easily precious things could be taken away from you, just like those golden rays of sun and just like those pretty flowers that would eventually wither and die.

Leni grabs her phone and sticks her earphones in, locates her favourite sleep meditation, but just before the track loads, she hears shouts coming from down the street.

Alison. Again.

That woman is such a bloody bitch, Leni thinks.

She doesn't know how somebody as sweet and as kind as Rory can handle living with her. Or how those cutie kids sleep at night with a psycho for a mum.

Leni listens, one earphone out, as the couple fight, Alison's words shrill and Rory speaking in low, placating tones.

Another tear rolls down Leni's cheek, because she thinks about how great a dad Rory is, and how he is so deserving of love. He deserves a love as powerful and magical as what she and Tristan have.

A horrifying thought occurs to her.

What if Alison and Rory started out like Tristan and Leni?

What if all couples turn out like that in the end?

She shivers and draws her covers up and over her shoulders and rubs her soft fluffy blanket against her chin. No. Her parents are alright. In fact, they are probably the most sane and normal couple on the street.

Tristan's parents – Sam and Ollie – are pretty good too. Always smiling and laughing and sometimes even holding hands.

Leni shakes her head and shoves all thoughts of the doomed couple in the street aside, and stuffs the AirPod back into her ear and plays the meditation music. She's excited for sleep to come, excited for the morning light to stream in through her window. Because that meant another day with Tristan.

And Tristan meant everything to her.

She's only started drifting off to sleep when something thumps against her bedroom door. She slides beneath the covers and watches through a small gap between the doona cover and the bed, breath held, her pulse throbbing loudly in her ears, as the doorknob twists and her bedroom door flings open.

Two people spill into Leni's room and collapse to the floor, along with a stream of hallway light.

Two *half-naked* people.

Dad and... Samantha?!?

Confused as to why they've fallen into her room, and momentarily ignoring that they are missing key items of clothing, Leni is about to get up and help them to their feet when she hears low moans coming from her dad... as he, no, he can't be... as he starts moving his lips up Sam's pale neck – *Samantha,* Tristan's mum – working his way up to her mouth. Samantha groans and moves her hips in response.

Leni is trapped, frozen, horrified into muteness.

Oh God, they aren't just kissing... they're... oh God.

'Dad! What are you doing?' she says, finally finding her voice. 'What are you doing with Tristan's mum? Where's Mum?'

Samantha rolls onto her back and stares up at Leni with mascara smudged, glazed eyes. A frown briefly flits across her forehead.

'Oh, Leni, love. It's not what... it's not what it looks like.'

'Leni...' Nathan says, rubbing his forehead. 'Why are you home? I thought–'

'Get out!' Leni screams, frightened by the sudden grip fear has on her heart. 'Get out,' she shouts as the fear squeezes her heart again, extra tightly.

Leni scrambles out of bed, her head burning with rage. She kicks at her dad's legs until they scramble to their feet and stumble out, leaving a strong waft of booze in their wake.

She locks the door behind them and slides down and catches her breath while her heart races against her ribcage. The fear is long gone now. Rage has taken its place.

Her dad and *Sam.*

Her dad and Tristan's mum.

It has come, she thinks to herself. The bad moment she's been dreading. It is the grey clouds casting shadows across the flower bed all over again.

Nothing good ever lasts.

# 16

## *Rory*

Rory shuffles to the very edge of the queen bed he shares with his wife. He can't even stomach the smell of her, or the fact that she is lying next to him in bed with only a few inches of white Egyptian cotton between them. Even the steady rise and fall of her shoulders as she sleeps – so soundly after a fight that had probably awoken the entire street – annoyed the heck out of him. How can she feel content enough to sleep so peacefully when their marriage is on its last raggedy legs?

He thinks about the fight. Of Alison's face beneath the dull yellow streetlight, the cruel smile she wore while she informed Rory that she'd slept with Michael. How the sex had been 'mind-blowing' and that she wasn't sure that Rory would be able to satisfy her after it.

Rory had responded with laughter, the hysterical kind.

'Bullshit, Ali. You hate sex, you're too worried about smearing your makeup or breaking a nail.'

Those words had enraged Alison to the point that when they arrived home, she'd pushed him again, a light shove that had made him hit the door frame as they entered the house. It hadn't hurt physically. But it had certainly bruised his ego.

For a good half hour after the incident occurred, he kept trying to justify what had happened, telling himself that they'd both had a lot to drink. Maybe she'd just bumped him accidentally. Or perhaps he'd simply gotten in the way.

But here, alone in the dark – because with Alison he may as well be alone – there is nothing but the bare truth swirling through his brain. Over and over again he replays what happens and it's unmistakable.

Alison *had* shoved him.

And he'd simply taken the mistreatment without a word.

Like a coward.

What have I become?

Rory sits up in the dark and kicks off the sheets, and enters the bathroom, locking himself in. He winces at the harsh light radiating from the ceiling globe when he turns it on, and stares at himself in the mirror.

Shirtless and in his boxer shorts, he wonders what Naomi would think of him like this, semi-naked. Would she appreciate his lean muscles? He'd noticed, when they'd woken up to Laura crying in the garden, that Naomi had seemed reluctant to pull away from him. Those few seconds had made him feel desirable, needed, wanted – things he has sorely missed in his life because he certainly hasn't gotten them from Alison in a long while.

He can still remember how soft and warm Naomi felt against his body. Alison hadn't let him hug her in so long, he felt desperate for more now. Like an ex-addict who's just relapsed because he got a taste of what affection is like. He thought he'd forgotten.

Naomi, he thinks... she's so beautiful, so smart, so kind – and so very sexy.

He pictures her full lips, those dark brown eyes of hers, the kind that penetrate your soul.

Though he'd never ever betray Alison by being with another woman, there's no harm in fantasising.

Closing his eyes, his thinks of his neighbour and slips his hands into his boxers.

But stops when the door handle jiggles.

'Rory? Open... geez... open the b-bloody door. Wha... what are you doing in there?'

Alison.

He opens his eyes and the harsh, glare of the bathroom light along with Alison's incessant banging on the door, and the fact that he is standing over the sink with his hands down his pants makes him feel so cold and alone. He shivers, taking his time to wash his hands before unlocking the door.

Alison pushes past him without saying a word, and proceeds to vomit into the toilet. She's had too many drinks, again. Rory can't remember a single gatho where his wife has learned when to stop.

He escapes the bathroom and shudders as he listens to her heaving. The sound of the contents of her stomach hitting the bowl, enough to make him dry retch.

A sharp acidic smell invades the bedroom.

Rory breathes through his mouth and stares at the crumpled bed sheets.

He thinks about his kids, about how much he misses their smiling faces and cheery natures. It's only the late hour that stops him from hopping into the car to drive to his in-laws and pick them up right now. He's only had two beers – he'd refused the pre key party vodka shots. But of course, he won't. They deserve a peaceful, fun sleepover. They don't need to come home just to comfort their miserable dad.

In the darkness of the bedroom, Rory sighs.

If it wasn't for the kids, would he be long gone by now? He thinks of this a lot and it often keeps him up late at night. Is he putting the kids through undue strain by forcing them to live with warring parents? Are he and Alison damaging them? Ruining their adult relationships through what they're seeing now?

He stuffs a pillow under his arm and heads to his oldest kid's bedroom. Once there he falls into the single bed and pulls the Buzz Lightyear doona cover over himself. The cool night air tickles his bare feet where the doona doesn't reach.

His mind instantly returns to Alison. The old Alison. The one the kids could laugh unabashedly in front of, without awaking anger. The one he could sneak up behind in the kitchen and tickle until she melted into a pool of breathless giggles in his arms.

Thinking of this Alison hurts his heart. He yearns for her. Pines for her as though grieving for a wife who has passed away.

And he suddenly decides that their marriage is worth saving. That his beautiful wife is in there somewhere. He'll just have to try to reach her. Help her. Ask her what's wrong. Ask her if there's anything that *he* can do, any changes *he* can make.

He wonders if he'll have the balls to speak up about the way she's been treating him. At the very least he will tell her that he isn't going to take any of her verbal or physical abuse anymore. That he is making a stand. That he has standards for himself and he doesn't deserve to be treated like crap anymore.

But deep down, he wonders if he does deserve it. He wonders if he sends out subconscious waves of useless, hopeless vibes her way that she can't help but treat him like crap. He's read plenty about it. How people only treat you the way that you allow them to.

He reaches across for the stuffed toy on the bedside table, the one his son forgot to take along to the sleepover, and he hugs it to his chest. The thought of seeing the kids tomorrow soothes his sorrow and sends his breath into an easy rhythm.

He'll take them out for fish and chips on the beach, they can run around and get their feet wet in the shore, build sandcastles while he clears his head and who knows...

Who the hell knows?

Maybe tomorrow will be the day that things begin to change.

# 17

## *Orlando*

Orlando wakes up, his mouth as dry as the Great Sandy Desert and his head thumping something chronic. While his mind proceeds to replay last night's events in a scary, rapidly flickering montage of mental images, he reaches out for the comfort and security of his wife's warm body. No matter what happened last night, Samantha is his best friend. They will talk it out, go over it all, widen their eyes, shake their heads and maybe laugh a little at what went on the night before and then say, 'never again'.

But the space that should be filled with Sam's warm body is empty, the sheets cold from not having been slept in.

Orlando's pulse thumps loudly against his eardrums.

He sits up and stares at Samantha's side of the bed, still neatly tucked in and his breath catches in his dry throat.

Sam didn't come home last night.

What. The. Fuck.

He releases his breath and takes a moment to calm himself down.

Okay. So, Sam slept at Laura's – big deal. Those two probably wanted to dissect the night's events over coffee into the early hours. Samantha also would have wanted to reassure Laura that she didn't sleep with her husband Nathan. That's why she stayed. It makes perfect sense now. Solidarity with her friend.

Orlando is feeling better already, despite his hangover.

His wife will probably walk in the door soon and maybe they can go out and get breakfast together, and she can fill him in on all the scandalous details of who was with whom and what they all did.

Throwing off the sheet and doona, he heads straight to the bathroom and turns on the shower. As soon as he strips off his clothes and steps under the warm water, he feels so much better. Everything is going to be okay. He knows that now. Feels it.

He starts to think back to last night. How Laura had 'chosen' his keys and how she hadn't wanted a bar of him until they'd heard Samantha and Nathan giggling in the next room. Then, after another bottle of wine and some casual banter, she had begun to really relax in Orlando's company.

'Let's just chat about sex,' she'd said, her cheeks turning red under the soft glow of her daughter's bedroom lamp. 'I could never actually betray Nathan. So, sex talk is the most I can offer.'

'That's completely fine by me,' Ollie had answered quickly, his shoulders relaxing with relief. Because for all his talk about wanting to do this key party, when it came to the crunch, there was no way he'd ever betray Samantha. She is the love of his life and seeing her disappear upstairs with Nathan, well, that had sent fiery jealousy shooting through his veins.

He still feels it now when he thinks about it. It makes him feel ill, his hangover returning with a vengeance.

But for all the giggles coming from the room next to them, he is still confident that Samantha wouldn't have actually engaged in any actual sexual activities. She would have potentially talked sex, flirted with the idea... but she was so against the idea when it was first mentioned, there is no way she would have gone through with it.

Ollie rinses the shampoo out of his hair and thinks about Laura again.

She surprised him last night when they'd discussed sex. He's known her for years and had always considered her sweet and maybe even a little vanilla. But when she had started talking about how she 'likes it rough', Orlando nearly spat out his drink all over Laura's daughter's pink doona.

It blows his mind that you don't truly ever know someone. That beneath the mask everyone presents to the world lie secret desires some are ashamed to admit.

Orlando thinks about his own desires and as he soaps his body, he is surprised to find himself thinking of Laura immediately. He can't ever remember feeling attracted to her. Not in that way anyway. He's always looked to her like a sister or a cousin. It's her mum that has always gotten him hot and bothered with the strange kinky milf vibe she's got going on.

But now, he can't stop thinking about Laura, and what she said she likes to do in the bedroom.

Steam fills the bathroom and Orlando begins to feel dizzy and so turns off the hot and keeps the cold on, letting the freezing water blast against his chest and face.

When he turns it off, he is grateful to find that the cool blast has eased the thumping in his head. He feels half-decent despite drinking so much booze.

But after drying off and getting dressed, the head-thumping returns and a dark sense of dread weighs upon his shoulders.

Samantha.

He needs to see Samantha.

Needs to hug her and kiss her, and tell her how much he loves her, and that they never need speak of key parties ever again.

Then he can shove Laura and her sexy little rough fantasies in a faraway corner of his brain.

And everything will then return to normal.

That's all he's ever wanted, he suddenly realises.

Normality.

A normal, boring, but happy life.

# 18

## *Laura*

I bury my toes in the cool beach sand and watch the waves roll in beneath dark, moody clouds.

What has our lovely, friendly, family-centric street become? What have *I* become? I feel dirty for even having hosted such a thing. My house and our minds all need bleaching. Have we ruined our lives forever? I'm not sure that I'll ever feel as cosy and safe and content in my home as I did before the key party happened.

Though the weather has only just decided to start behaving like autumn, with a sudden drop in temperature and the winds picking up, I stand and unwrap my scarf. Next, I take off my hoodie, T-shirt and tights, tossing them to the sand in one big tangle, and kick off my sneakers and peel off my socks.

In only my lacy bra and underwear, I brave the biting wind and the stinging sand which whips at my goose-prickled skin as I stride out into the sea, with hopes that the water will cleanse me of this revolting feeling crawling all over my skin.

Icy cold water inches its way up my bare thighs and though I bristle at the temperature, I relish it too. The sharp sting of the water brings me out of my head, out of the bedroom with Orlando, out of the moment I watched Nathan happily disappear up the stairs with my friend Samantha. For just a moment, I'm here, standing in freezing water, my eyes on a distant horizon where the rest of the world exists, reminding me that we are small, that we are an insignificant part of something so much larger.

A seagull screeches to my right and lands in the water two metres away, where it sits and bobs around in the wavy water. Little beady eyes watch me and for a moment I wish I could be that little cute seagull. I'd fly around in the vast sky all day, the jewel-coloured Indian Ocean beneath me, diving for fish and occasionally stealing chips from the humans.

'You're so lucky, little guy,' I say, and the bird draws its head back as if to say 'how dare you' and takes flight, giving me one last screech before it soars up and joins its mates.

Dipping my trembling hands into the ocean, I splash cold, salty water against my face and inhale the tangy, briny scent of the sea. The sea always reminds me of my childhood. Only happy things happen by the sea. Swimming, jumping off the jetty, watermelon slices, dripping red icy poles, fish and chips, the sleepy, drug-like stupor, the pure exhaustion you feel in the warm car on the way home, feeling safe in the knowledge that you're with your family and your parents will get you home safe.

Tears come as the memory of last night's events return with a vengeance.

Even though I did nothing physical with Orlando, guilt still consumes me and gives me that horrible prickly feeling running down my neck.

Not because I betrayed Nathan, because I didn't. But because I betrayed *myself*. I told Orlando things I'd never shared with anyone. They were my secrets, my private thoughts. Just for me.

And now I've handed those private details over to my neighbour, one of my closest friends' husband.

My stomach churns much like the waves in the sea and my face burns with shame. How will I ever look Orlando in the eye again? How will I look Samantha in the eye? The fact that I even spoke to her husband about my sexual preferences, just feels wrong. I hope she'll forgive me. She was so against this from the get-go and I have a feeling her sudden change of mood last night, her eagerness to join in on the key party, was only due to those vodka shots and all the wine she'd drunk.

I shake my head and dive into the sea, allowing the icy cold water to take me, to swallow me whole.

If only I could stay here, underwater, where the world is silent.

If only Nathan hadn't disappeared upstairs with Samantha, one of my closest friends, with so much enthusiasm. And even though I know that Sam would never do anything with Nathan, just knowing that Nathan wanted it is enough to tarnish our marriage forever.

I'd rushed out the door this morning, after waking up outside on the loveseat, a thick blanket covering me. Naomi and Rory must have covered me up.

The neighbour's cat had woken me up with his hungry wails and after giving him a few scraps of ham, I'd grabbed my car keys without stopping to check on Nathan.

I had to get out of the house.

But now what? I'll have to face it sometime.

Shivering violently, I dive right back into the choppy water, grey from the gathering dark clouds, and when I emerge, I feel warmth against my face and open my eyes to the clouds parting ever so slightly to allow a single streak of sunlight to beam down upon my face.

For just a few seconds, I'm back in the moment, enjoying the simplicity of nature, before I dive into the sea again, desperately trying to cling to the peaceful feeling that nature gives me.

The sand at the bottom of the ocean remains unstirred, despite its churning surface, and I wonder if I can be more like that sand. If I can remain calm and still while chaos erupts around me.

The minutes pass and the ocean, as it always does, works its charm, because when I finally emerge from the water and return to my pile of hastily discarded clothes, I feel somewhat revived.

I'm not sure how I'll explain to my parents why I'm a sopping wet, sandy mess when I pick up the boys, but that's the least of my problems.

Once I have the boys with me, I'll pick up Leni from the library where she has arranged to study with Tristan, and we can all go out for a nice lunch at our favourite cafe which has a playground within the grounds. While the boys play, I can have a nice girlie chat with Leni, and find out how things are going between her and Tristan.

As I tiptoe quickly to my car, I shiver like mad, the sharp gravel of the carpark digs into my bare soles, and the wind batters my wet ears, making them ache.

But I feel alive.

I feel good.

I smile to myself and a little girl seated in the idling car parked beside me, all wrapped up in a beach towel, looks at me curiously through the window and then beams me a huge smile before her parents drive her away.

My heart warms.

You've got today.

You've got this moment.

This is what matters.

Now.

The past is gone, the future is not here yet.

The cool sand between my toes, the golden sun peeking through the angry clouds, that child's smile and the knowledge that I'll be hugging my children soon, makes everything okay.

For now.

# 19

### *Naomi*

Naomi smiles to herself as a familiar door knock echoes through her house. The kids emerge from their rooms and start tearing down the hallway towards the front door, screaming with joy.

It's the Pavlovian response. They practically salivate for the little chocolate egg with the toy inside that they know they'll get from their uncles – Naomi's baby brother and his husband Jakov.

She opens the front door and is predictably greeted by her brother Aiden with a quick, awkward hug. He's always been this way, so shy and reserved, since he was a little boy. But his husband, Jakov, opens his arms wide for a bear hug and squeezes her tight, before kissing her on both cheeks, as is the Croatian way she's come to know and love.

In his hands is a plate of his famous palačinke, that he refuses to share the recipe for. He jokes that she'll never invite him over again as he'll no longer be needed.

She takes the warm plate of delectable rolled crepes filled with jam and heads into the kitchen while Aiden and Jakov endure the kids jumping all over them and shoving their sticky hands in their pockets while searching for the eggs they know their uncles have brought them.

Naomi laughs to herself as she puts the kettle on. This visit is exactly what she needs. A distraction from last night. The soccer game early this morning had been a pretty good diversion too. A diversion from her increasingly inappropriate thoughts about Rory.

As the sound of the boiling kettle fills the room, and Naomi is once again left alone with her thoughts, she can't help but think about all the shouting in the street last night. She'd been drifting off to sleep when the peace of the night was suddenly invaded by Alison screaming at Rory. For the next ten minutes she'd lain stiffly in bed, barely breathing as she'd listened to what sounded at first like Alison arguing with herself, until she finally heard, just barely, the low, quiet tones of Rory trying to appease his wife.

The fight made Naomi think about that letter she'd found and had finally read last night, the letter in which Rory had 'confessed' to Alison that he'd never really been there for her and how he wished that he could turn back time and help her face whatever secret demons she was battling on her own.

As she gets the milk out the fridge, Naomi wonders about Rory and Alison's relationship.

You never truly know what goes on behind closed doors and now, after having read the letter, she feels guilty for judging Alison as the complete bitch who bullies her husband. Naomi really knows nothing about her. Nothing beneath the surface anyway. She wonders if she should invite Alison over for a coffee or a wine one evening, get to know her a little better. She could be going through something and be in need of a friend. Yes, Naomi decides. I will reach out to Alison.

Naomi will never forget, after David passed, the mysterious box of fresh fruit and vegetables delivered to her doorstep each week. It went on for two months before she found out that it was Alison who had been behind it. And although Alison refused to accept any form of thanks, and had waved away Naomi's bunch of thank-you flowers citing allergies, Naomi will never forget the kindness behind that gesture.

The kettle's now boiled and Naomi gets out three green ceramic mugs, hand-made by her auntie, an artist who lives in the Northern Territory, and sets them on the counter.

She thinks of her own relationship with David, of what it had been like between them. They'd been two completely different people with completely different personalities, and yet they'd lived in harmony with one another.

David with his love of cars and engines and anything mechanical and Naomi with her love of art and nature.

Gosh they had loved each other. With such a depth it frequently brought physical pain to her heart when she thought of the gaping hole his passing left behind in her life.

She'd been full with David. Content. The kids had perfectly added to that fullness. But now she felt that great void and yes, the kids had helped to fill it, but she missed the companionship of an adult. Sure, she had the entire street to chat to and confide in, but she missed having somebody just for her.

It had been so lovely to speak to Rory last night. To listen and be listened to.

Just thinking about Rory now, and the way that he'd held her last night is enough to start butterflies stirring in her tummy. But riding on the wings of those butterflies is guilt. Guilt for even considering another man when her husband has only been gone for five years. And guilt because Rory has a wife. Sure, that wife is rather loud and rude, but she is still, as we speak, his wife, and Naomi will take no part in tearing that marriage apart. That is, if it isn't torn to shreds already.

No.

Rory is out of bounds.

She stares out the window, glimpsing one of the trees from Rory and Alison's backyard in the distance, its branches getting tossed about in the strong winds. He hasn't pruned it yet and he normally does all his pruning before Easter time, which has been and gone.

'Ooh, she's staring into space, Aiden. I know that look,' says Jakov conspiratorially.

Naomi blinks and realises that she's zoned out the entire time it took her kids to pry the chocolate eggs from her brother and brother-in-law's pockets. She rolls her eyes at her brother-in-law's cheeky comment.

'The weather's gone crazy, hasn't it? Looks like a storm's coming,' she says, biting her lip.

'And a change of subject. Well. I want a name, height, and occupation and a rating out of ten.' Jakov winks. 'Personality-wise of course, get your head out of that superficial gutter, Naomi,' he says, tutting.

Now it's Aiden's turn to roll his eyes along with Naomi. But a smile plays on his lips and he slips an arm around his husband with such affection that Naomi cannot help the sudden emotion that floods her. Watching her brother get married to the man that he loves last year, in front of all the family and friends, was one of the happiest days of her life. She just wished that David could have been alive to see it too.

Her eyes begin to sting with tears and she quickly turns and sticks her head in the pantry, quickly wiping them as she digs around for a packet of biscuits. Note to self, never to mix vodka and wine again. She'd forgotten how weepy it makes her the next day.

'Okay, so coffee or tea?'

'Coffee,' says Aiden. 'Buckets of it and about half a tonne of sugar.' He grins. 'I've got work this arvo.'

I laugh.

'Remember when Mum made you drink an entire cup of sugar diluted with just a bit of hot water?'

He widens his eyes.

'Oh gosh, yes! I'd forgotten about that. She thought forcing me to have too much was going to stop me from being a sugar addict.'

'It clearly didn't work,' says Jakov, sighing dramatically and turning his head as though insulted. 'I think he married me just for my sweetness.'

Naomi and Aiden look at each other and burst out laughing.

Aiden gives Jakov a playful slap on the arm. 'You know it.'

Naomi, still smiling, holds up a box of tea and shakes it, while looking at Jakov with raised brows.

'Yep, tea for me. Coffee gets me so wired and I plan on just lounging around in bed all day just reading, eating and sleeping. I'm so tired. Urgh. Work is killing me.' He sighs and rests an arm on Aiden's shoulder.

Aiden massages the back of Jakov's shoulders and steers him towards the soft brown couches in the living room.

'I think we need to get comfy. Is it okay if we have our drinks in here?' says Aiden.

'Sure. I'll be just a minute.'

Naomi's heart practically bursts with pride for these two. They've both worked so hard at building a future together, committing themselves to owning their own home before they bring children into their lives. They want to be ready – financially, emotionally and physically – so that they can give the children they adopt the best life possible.

But in the meantime, they are the best damn uncles in the country, if not the world, she thinks, grinning to herself.

Naomi's kids adore them, so much so, she has to sometimes shoo them away or bribe them with a movie just so she and Aiden and Jakov can have some time together to chat.

Naomi feels desperate to offload what went on last night. Aiden will likely get embarrassed. He's always felt awkward discussing sex in front of her, just a brotherly thing. But Jakov is always up for sex talk, so she knows that he's going to respond with enthusiastic interest.

They sip their hot drinks and discuss work for a while before Naomi sighs and figures she won't be able to concentrate on anything else until she spills the beans.

'Okay, so... you know how we all catch up every fortnight in this street?'

Jakov raises his brows. 'Ooooh yes... I'm sensing something juicy. What's happened now? Is it Nathan and Laura or is it that Alison woman with that lovely, sexy husband of hers?'

Aiden raises his brows at his husband and Jakov responds with, 'Of course he's not as sexy as you, my love.'

Aiden smiles. 'Okay, so maybe he is a little bit sexy.'

Naomi feels herself blush at the mention of Rory's sexiness and she immediately regrets it because Jakov and Aiden share a look and a laugh and soon Jakov is leaning forward, cradling his tea in his hand saying, 'Oh my God, you have a sneaky crush on him, haven't you?'

Naomi swats his words away like an invisible fly.

'Shush. No. Listen, you two are not going to believe this... and no judgement please... because I just kind of went along with it... I didn't really actually want to partici–'

'Just spit it out already.'

Naomi nods, sets her coffee down on the coffee table and presses her palms against her knees.

'Okay, so I may have attended a swinger party at Laura and Nathan's house last night.'

She releases the sentence in one long exhalation and sits back to watch the various expressions grow and evolve on her brother and brother-in-law's faces.

'What?' says Aiden, blinking several times, a habit which he has not been able to shake since he was little. 'What on earth, Naomi?'

Jakov who is sitting open-mouthed and wide-eyed, finally leans forward and gently slaps her on the knee.

'You need to tell us *everything*. I want detail upon detail.'

'What in the heck, Naomi? I mean what the hell?' says Aiden again, swearing under his breath.

'Shush,' says Jakov. 'Let her tell us.'

'Okay, so. A couple of weeks ago, we were at Nathan and Laura's house and Laura told us all how her mother revealed that back in the seventies they used to have these parties where everyone tossed their keys into the fruit bowl and the women plucked the keys and went with whomever they'd chosen and had sex.'

Aiden shakes his head, his old-fashioned sensibilities clearly disgusted, while Jakov leans forward, intent on hearing more juicy details.

'Well, Alison decided to write up these rules and she read them out last night and then suddenly we were doing this thing.'

'You were at a key party last night?' Aiden says, shaking his head again. 'That's so tacky and so... unlike you.'

'Hear me out. I didn't sleep with anyone and the rules are that you can just chat, cuddle or whatever, the point being to spend time with somebody else and I guess go home more appreciative of your partner. I'm not one hundred percent sure if that was everybody's intention, but anyway. Those were the rules.'

'Whose keys did you get?' Jakov asks.

Naomi glances from her brother to Jakov.

'Guess.' She feels herself blush again.

'OMG, you got Rory?'

Aiden's eyes widen. 'Rory?' he says, mimicking his husband, his excitement overriding his disgust. 'So, what happened?'

'Tell me you at least did *something* with that gorgeous man,' says Jakov.

'Jakov!' Naomi widens her eyes at him and laughs. 'I didn't do anything sexual with him.' A giggle tickles her throat. 'We actually fell asleep in each other's arms out on a loveseat in the backyard.'

'That's actually so sweet,' says Jakov, a dreamy look in his blue eyes.

'Yeah, it is pretty cute. But it seems wrong still,' says Aiden, leaning forward and gnawing on his nails.

'We just sat together and chatted while everyone disappeared into the bedrooms.'

'Rory suggested we just talk or cuddle and I chose to cuddle with him and chat.' Naomi smiles, because she can't help but smile when thinking about Rory and last night, and sits back against the couch, crossing her feet at her ankles. 'Don't make me feel guilty, Aiden, because I thoroughly enjoyed it. I've missed that, just being held. It was wonderful.'

Aiden's face softens and his eyes shine with emotion. He's always been so easily moved. Her sweet, soft, baby brother.

'Well, that's certainly not tacky. And I'm glad you got to do that. You need it. Everyone needs comfort. As long as it goes no further than a hug though.'

She understands her brother's resistance to all of this. Rory is a married man and Aiden is fiercely triggered when it comes to cheating due to a previous relationship where he was hurt by a serial cheater – which of course happened while he was under the spotlight already for publicly outing himself as gay, at the height of his career as a star Indigenous AFL player.

'Oh gosh, Aiden, I know he's married, that's why I would never even consider it.'

'But don't you think the cuddle is cheating already?'

Naomi stares into the large wide brown eyes of her brother and nods. 'In a sense, yes, but Alison quite happily walked away with Michael so… I don't know. I think Rory kind of deserved a hug and a chat. And look, we're just friends.'

'Michael?' says Jakov. 'Aren't they high school buddies?'

Naomi shakes her head and swallows down the last gulp of her coffee.

'No. You're thinking of Samantha – they've known each other for years. No. She got Nathan. And I have a funny feeling that maybe…'

'What? They actually slept together?' asks Aiden.

Jakov reaches across and covers Aiden's hand with his own, entwining his olive-toned fingers with Aiden's brown ones. The gesture seems to work and Aiden relaxes back into the couch, the throbbing vein in his temple gone.

'Did Rory at any time ask you for sex?' asks Jakov. 'I need way more details than you're providing here.'

Naomi can't help the smile creeping up as she pictures Rory asleep in her arms, looking so innocent and so exhausted.

'No. Of course not. He's a perfect gentleman.'

'So, he's one of the good ones,' says Jakov, nodding.

'I bet he wanted to, though,' says Aiden, his jaw stiffening and the muscles beneath his shirt tensing up. 'And that's still an intention to cheat in my eyes.'

'Well, he was kind enough not to ask. So, it says what kind of a man he is. Plus, he said that he hasn't had sex in over a year. Gets no affection from his wife. So, considering all of that…' Naomi shakes her head. 'I also saw her shove him the other day, out the front of the house. I looked away and pretended I didn't see it. I felt horrible afterwards. I mean, just because he's a guy, doesn't mean I shouldn't step in and help, right? If it were a woman, then I probably would've said something. But I didn't. So anyway, I felt pretty bad about that. I feel pretty shit about it, to tell you the truth.' She bends her head to take a sip of her coffee, only to find none left.

'Marriage or not, that man deserves some love.' Jakov cradles his tea. 'I think, under the current circumstances, a little bit of attention from you can't be considered cheating, surely? I can't believe he hasn't had sex in over a year. Geez, he'd last all of about five seconds.'

Aiden sighs, gets up and heads into the kitchen.

Naomi and Jakov listen out as Aiden turns on the tap and rinses his mug out and places it on the sink.

'Great. I've upset him,' says Jakov, sighing. 'I should have been a bit more sensitive. But gosh, poor Rory though,' he says, lowering his voice. 'He deserves some love, Naoms. Imagine not having sex for over a year and yet still sharing a bed with your partner night after night?' He raises his brows at Naomi. 'And what about you? You deserve some affection too. You've been alone for so bloody long.'

'He's married, Jakov.'

'Of course. I get that... and gosh, this doesn't mean I have a cheating bone in my body. I'm a one-man man. But Rory... I feel for the guy. I really do. I feel for you too.'

Naomi doesn't know what to say to that so instead she stands.

They both go into the kitchen to join Aiden.

Naomi thinks about Rory and how he'd hung his head after Alison had shoved him. How diminished he must have felt in that moment, and she suddenly wishes she'd kissed him last night, given him at least some kind of intimate affection. Not that she wanted to cheat or steal him away. It's more that she wants to give him *something*. To make him feel wanted and loved.

Her cheeks warm again and Jakov wags a finger at her, which makes Aiden, who is now being swamped by the kids for hugs, smile again.

Naomi stands and draws her stiff brother into her arms and pats him on the back, squeezing him until he softens his resistance and melts against her body.

'Love you, Naoms,' he says, before kissing her on the forehead. 'See you at Mum's next week.'

'Yeah. Should be fun.' She smiles and sighs with a sense of relief. 'I'm so glad I have you guys.'

She hugs Jakov, his warm hug soothing her troubled soul.

'Now we want detailed updates on any more parties. When's the next one?' Jakov asks eagerly.

Naomi shrugs. She doesn't think there'll be a next one. She certainly hopes she never hears the term 'key party' ever again, for all the trouble and drama it brings with it.

She waits for the kids to run ahead out the front door.

'Who knows. I'd say that everyone will be over it after last night. Laura was crying, so... I don't know, unless everyone wants a divorce, I doubt a key party will ever happen again.'

Aiden nods, as though relieved to not have to consider so many couples cheating on each other.

Naomi and the kids wave Aiden and Jakov off out the front and while out there, she notices the absence of Rory's car from his driveway. It's been gone since early this morning and she feels a twinge of guilt when a tiny thrill tickles her stomach at the prospect of Rory and Alison splitting up.

She shakes her head. No. She doesn't want their marriage to end. She wants them to fix it, so that Rory can be happy with the woman he so obviously loves.

She wants Alison to be happy too. And to come to her senses and treat Rory with the respect that he deserves, that everyone deserves.

But Naomi isn't going to feel guilty about enjoying the feel of Rory's arms around her last night, or the fact that he'd acknowledged David when everybody else treated his memory like an elephant in the room.

She's allowed to think about Rory, isn't she? Allowed to fantasise? She can appreciate him from afar. No harm will come from that.

'Can we do the park with everyone today?' asks Layla, jumping up and down on the spot, the sugar from the chocolate egg Aiden and Jakov had brought zooming through her little veins.

Going to the park on a Sunday is somewhat of a neighbourhood ritual. But when Naomi casts her gaze up and down the street, she notes the drawn blinds of Nathan and Laura's, the absence of Rory's car, and Michael's, and concludes, with a small shiver, that for today at least, there will be no catch-up at the park.

# 20

### *Michael*

Michael stands in the shower, hot water streaming down his body, one hand on his slick, wet body and the other resting against the cool, wet tiles.

He screws his eyes shut and pictures Alison as she'd been last night when they'd disappeared into the spare bedroom at Laura and Nathan's house – topless.

It had been a long time since he'd seen a naked woman in the flesh and even if she hadn't wanted to be touched and had insisted on giving him a hand-job only, and despite the hand-job being so clinical it could well have been performed by his elderly male GP, the sight of those magnificent breasts had been enough to make it totally worth his while.

In his fantasy, he erases the look of mild disgust she'd worn while she'd jacked him off, and instead replaces it with lusty eyes and shiny kiss-me lips.

It doesn't take him long to finish, and as always, exhaustion follows, as well as a subtle feeling of bleakness.

Loneliness sucks.

He knows that once he steps out of the shower, he'll face another solo evening in front of the telly with a glass of wine his only company.

At least he eats well. He always cooks himself a meal from scratch even if it's just a BLT or a steak sandwich.

Once in the kitchen, the bleakness hits him hard. He stares out of his kitchen window where he can see Naomi's rooftop, and it bums him out that she, a beautiful, intelligent, single woman, is only a few houses away, with an empty space beside her in her warm bed, and her children in need of a father figure, not that he would ever in a million years imagine himself replacing David.

She'd said no when he'd asked her to dinner again, in the earlier part of the evening last night, before all that swinger shit went down, and he'd felt such a fool for having been turned down twice.

The strange thing is, he's always thought of his best friend Samantha as the one that got away. He wonders what would have happened had Sam drawn Michael's keys last night. He's known her for so long and has loved her for so long. What if they had been paired up and had ended up sleeping together? A marriage could have been ruined.

He shakes his head and rinses off some vegetables he'd dug out of the bottom of the fridge. The capsicum has seen better days.

Sometimes he just wants to forget it all. Forget the search for a special someone in his life and just enjoy his life as it is.

Because he does have it pretty good. His own house, enough money to go on holiday anywhere he wants. A good bunch of friends he gets to catch up with fortnightly and anytime in between.

But now he wonders what the mood will be the next time they all get together, that's if they do at all for a while.

He knows that Alison and Rory had engaged in one of their legendary screaming matches last night – with more screams than usual. He can just picture Alison torturing Rory with every minute detail of her encounter with him.

Michael shudders a little as he slices away the mushy, rotten part of the green capsicum. Last night was just plain wrong. He wonders if he should find Rory later on and apologise to him. But then he remembers Alison's rules about not sharing details of what happened on the night to anyone.

He'd seen Samantha in the early hours of the morning, before dawn, the sky apricot and milky blue, as she crossed the lawns doing the walk of shame, her long, curly blonde hair a mess, her eyes dark and hollow. She'd indicated that she'd message him later but his phone hasn't lit up once since last night. He's not exactly sure what went on between her and Nathan, but he imagines the mood would be pretty grim in her house at the moment judging by how she'd looked in those early hours.

He takes out the whole barbeque chicken he'd purchased at Woolworths the day before and proceeds to remove the cooked white flesh and chop it up. Next, he whisks some eggs and makes an omelette. He puts it aside, then adds chopped onion to a hot pan, sliced carrots and sugar snap peas. Then comes the chopped chicken and two handfuls of softened rice noodles.

A bit of soy sauce and some honey finishes the job.

He tips it all into a large spaghetti bowl, jams in a fork, pours himself a wine with his left hand, leaving the cap off, then carries it through to the living room where his faithful, worn-in couch awaits him, complete with books ready to read on the arm.

He smiles to himself, thinking about the crime novel he'll get stuck into tonight.

Rain, and a howling wind, begins to batter against the windowpane and he recalls the news predicting a dramatic change of weather this week. For once the news is right.

The food is tasty, the wine heavy and dry, just the way he likes it. The rain continues to pour and he listens to the noisy patter it makes against his tin roof while he chews and swallows.

Yeah. He has it pretty good. The embarrassing knock-back from Naomi slowly fades into the past as he enjoys the effects of the wine warming his blood.

He spoons in the last mouthful of stir-fry, sucking up the saucy noodles, and groans. Another gulp of wine and he is a happy man. Maybe he'll even crack open a beer or two later.

While the rain lashes at his windows, he washes the wok, cutlery and spaghetti bowl and is about to pour another wine when his phone, which is resting on the counter beside the sink, lights up and then turns black again. Then it lights up again with a second message, then a third. His phone has never experienced so much activity in one night let alone a handful of seconds.

He grabs it with wet hands, knocking over the uncapped wine bottle in the process.

He swears, but lets the wine leach out all over his cream tiles.

Samantha has written.

He hurriedly opens the messages.

*Shit Michael, I need to come over.*
*Now.*
*If that's okay.*
*I fucked up.*
*Please write back!!!*

Michael stares longingly at his unopened crime novel, and regretfully at the spilled wine, but shakes his head and quickly texts Samantha a reply. His best mate needs him. He'll do anything for her. That's how it works between them. She's always been there for him too.

'Yeah, come now,' he writes, adding a smiley in case she needs a friendly face.

He feels guilty for thinking it because Samantha is in obvious distress, but this is the most excitement he's had in ages.

Sam needs him.

His phone lights up again.

> *Thanks, Michael. Thanks for being my*
> *one true friend*
> *Coming now*

# 21

## *Samantha*

Samantha's rain-soaked hair clings to her cheeks and her teeth chatter as she stands shivering on Michael's front doorstep, staring at the brown leaves which have collected beneath the doormat.

She knocks on his door and her mind goes straight back to last night. It's all she can think about. The look on Leni's face... that is something that Samantha will never forget. Her stomach churns and her head thumps as she closes her eyes to the memory in a futile attempt to shut it out.

This can't be real. How could she have been so stupid, to have single-handedly ruined so many lives over one stupid, messy and quite frankly, rather unsatisfying sexual encounter with her friend's husband.

She wants to turn back time. She wants to shake her head at Alison's rules and side with Laura, and echo her friend's protests against what they were about to do.

Tears spring to Samantha's eyes as soon as Michael opens his front door and lets her inside. The look in his eyes, the kindness and the lack of judgement there, has her sobbing by the time she's made it into his living room.

'Something smells good,' she says between gasps of air and sobs. Not that she's hungry. In fact, she'd rather not eat for the rest of her life and just waste away until she disappears. Because she can't imagine partaking in the simple pleasure of eating ever again. She can't imagine anything being normal again.

'Stir-fry. Unfortunately, I've eaten it all,' he says, patting his flat belly which refuses to put on weight despite Samantha always seeing Michael stuff his face.

'But I can whip you something up super-quick. A toasted sanger or a BLT?'

Samantha shakes her head as the weight of what she did last night with Nathan causes her to sway on her feet. Michael steadies her and gently guides her to his soft, worn couch that smells so much like him – like books and wine and beer and food. She collapses against the soft padding with a thud and contemplates staying here on this couch forever, until she dies from the crushing guilt that is squeezing the air from her lungs.

Michael kneels before her, his warm, heavy hand covering hers in a gesture of comfort that only causes Samantha's heart to ache and the guilt to crush her even more. She doesn't deserve his kindness. She doesn't deserve anybody's kindness.

'I'm not hungry. I haven't eaten since last night – I can't stomach anything, not even coffee. I drank so much last night, oh *God*.' Tears blur her vision. She's cried so much the past few hours she isn't sure how she has any fluids left in her body. She feels like an empty husk, drained of everything.

'But all the alcohol in the world doesn't excuse what I've done. It'll never excuse it.' She meets Michael's gaze of concern. 'And the worst part is I remember. I remember it all. No. The worst part of it all is that I remember Leni… I remember poor Leni and the look on her face.' Samantha shakes her head. 'I've ruined her life. I've actually ruined that kid's life. Oh God, and I've ruined my son's life.' She wraps her arms around herself and starts rocking back and forth. 'I don't know what to do. When Tristan finds out he's going to hate me.'

Samantha watches, through stinging eyes, as Michael gets up to put the kettle on and drops a teabag into a teacup. Once it's brewed, he brings the steaming cup and a couple of crackers over to her.

'You can give me the proper details after you've had this tea and these crackers. Then we'll talk. It's chamomile.'

Samantha nods and takes it and slowly drinks the hot, sweet tea, her eyes taking in the new feminine touches Michael has added to his home. Touches she's never noticed before, at least, not on any of her recent visits. It must be very new.

The vase of red roses, the bright yellow and green tablecloth spread across the dining table beneath them, the scented candle sitting atop his unused fireplace, unlit of course and still in its pretty box.

'Wait a second. Is there something I should know, Michael? Do you have a girlfriend?' she asks suddenly, grateful for the momentary reprieve from the horror of what she's done.

Michael appears momentarily stumped, or perhaps confused by the question, but then she watches as his gaze shifts from the vase to the candle. She thinks she sees a light blush bloom in his tan cheeks.

'Nah. Just thought I'd spruce the place up.' He sighs before he bows his head. 'Actually, earlier on last night, before everything... well... anyway, I asked Naomi over for dinner, sometime next week, her kids too. But she said no.' He makes a face, like the cringe emoji, all teeth, the corners of his mouth going extreme sideways. 'And it's not the first time she's rejected me.'

Samantha feels her numb heart soften and slowly feel again, for Michael. After she'd woken up that morning in one of Laura and Nathan's boys' beds, she'd wanted to remain numb and unfeeling forever. But here she is again, opening herself up to an onslaught of fresh pain.

Oh God, here it comes again, she thinks. More flashbacks.

She recalls how horrified she'd felt, when she'd woken in Laura and Nathan's house, sunlight streaming in through the curtains. How she'd scrambled from the bed and let herself out of the house as little video-like flashes started assaulting her dehydrated brain.

Then the against-Alison's-rules phone call from Nathan, explaining to Samantha that he had made her stay over only because she'd threatened to kill herself after Leni had seen them together. That Samantha had wailed like a lunatic about how Tristan was going to hate her after he found out and how she may as well kill herself and save everyone the inconvenience of having to look at her shameful form ever again.

Concerned, Nathan had kept watch until eventually going to bed in the early hours of the morning.

Samantha feels horrible and hideous about that. She feels so bad for Laura. Fancy your own friend sleeping with your husband. It's unforgivable.

The tears come again, stinging her already raw eyes. She sets her trembling, half-drunk teacup on the arm of the couch and presses her palms against her eyes.

'Aww, come on, Sammy, come on. It can't be that bad,' says Michael, coming to sit beside her, making the couch sink. She falls towards him as he puts his arm around her shoulders and gives her a squeeze.

Samantha nods. 'It can, Michael, it really can. And it *is*. I slept with Nathan, the father of Tristan's girlfriend, the husband of one of my closest girlfriends. That's bad, Michael. That's plenty bad.'

Michael rubs her arm.

'Well, that's what everyone agreed to last night, remember? And you don't even have to speak to anybody about it. Those were the rules.' He sighs. 'Does Orlando know?'

'I haven't outright said it. And I suppose there's a chance he doesn't know. But I'm assuming he does. And if he does, he's being so strangely good about it,' she says, more tears spilling over. 'And that makes it worse. So much worse.'

'But if Orlando is okay with it, then what's wrong?'

Samantha takes several, great shuddering gulps of air.

'Leni came home early and we didn't know that she was in her room. We kind of stumbled in, fell on each other, half-naked and started engaging in the act...'

'Shit. Okay, when you say it like that. That is pretty bad. What did she do? What did *you* do?'

'She just froze at first, then she came over to us, I think to help us up. But then she saw... she saw what we were doing... then she screamed at us to get out. Then I... I got up and said something along the lines of, "Sorry, this isn't what it looks like," like some shitty movie line. Oh *God,* Michael, I'm such an idiot.'

Samantha clutches at her head and shakes it. Like a wave, the regret and the guilt rolls over her and crashes against her already bruised heart, again and again, squeezing at her lungs until she can't breathe.

Michael rubs her back until she calms down enough to speak again.

'I've fucked up, Michael. Big time. Leni will be traumatised for life, and, oh God, when Tristan finds out. He'll never speak to me again. He won't.'

Michael sighs softly.

'Of course he will. But you might have to allow him to process it in his own time. If he doesn't want to talk in the beginning then just give it time.'

She draws away from his comfort for a moment, as though she doesn't deserve it.

'Then I will kill myself. I seriously will. Because if I don't have my beautiful boy in my life, I don't have anything.'

Michael hugs Samantha again and makes comforting hush noises, like a mother does when she soothes her child.

'You know what? It's still the morning-after and I can guarantee you everyone is feeling like crap right now. Give it time. Leni might be so embarrassed she might not even mention it to Tristan. Who knows? She's a good kid. She might not want to hurt him like that, you know?'

Samantha nods. What he is saying is likely probable, but still. Leni shouldn't have to have this kind of thing weighing her down. She's only a kid for crying out loud. And Samantha has done this to her. Samantha has burdened a teenage girl with this very adult mess. Yes, Nathan had taken part in it all too. He is as much a part of this as Samantha. But right now, she sees this as her own problem. This is about her own stupid choice.

'I wanted to go over and say something, apologise, but I can't face Leni or Laura. I just don't know what to do. There's a Parents' Day coming up at school and I'll have to face the lot of them all at once. I don't know if I'll be able to do that. I don't know if I'll be able to show my face in public ever again.'

'Maybe that's for the best. Get it over with and then everyone will eventually move on and all of our lives will return to normal.'

Samantha nods, knowing this isn't true and knowing that their little idyllic street has just been ruined, bulldozed over by the stupid actions of a bunch of drunken adults.

She feels sick and so unclean she wants to take a bath in bleach until there is nothing left of her.

'What are you thinking?' Michael asks, his voice soft and filled with kindness.

She tells him about the bleach bath and he chuckles low and deep in his throat.

'Aww, Sammy. Trust me, you'll feel so much better about this tomorrow. You know, just because you're an adult doesn't mean you can't make any mistakes. You can be an eighty-year-old and still do stupid stuff. We're human, not bloody angels.'

She stares into his face, into his soft dark eyes, and realises that she has one of the best friends she could ever ask for. She's always known that Michael has kept a secret candle burning for her, but in all the years since he's moved into the street, he's never once mentioned it. That is the kind of gentleman he's always been.

'Thanks, Michael. I'm so glad you're here, in my life, in this street. I don't know what I'd do without you. If you'd turned your back on me after all of this, then I honestly would have probably tried to kill myself right now.'

'Oi, none of that talk. Think of Tristan. It'd be worse if you killed yourself. Imagine the last thing he knew about you was that you slept with Nathan. Look, and let's be realistic, he might not even find out about this. And maybe one day, when you're ninety-six and on your deathbed, you'll say, "I've got a confession to make..." and you'll tell your grandkids about how you slept with your neighbour, Nathan, and they'll be scandalised but laugh it off because they'll think, wow, Nana, you naughty little minx you.' He grins. 'Or they'll just think you're senile.'

Samantha laughs at the mental image and almost wishes she is already ninety-six years of age so that she could get this hideous secret off her chest and tell the truth to her only child, the greatest love of her life, and to also apologise to Orlando and promise to never do anything like this again.

She sighs and wipes away her tears and uses Michael's bathroom to attempt to splash some of the redness away from her face.

While searching for a clean towel, she can't help but notice the bowl of floating candles, also unlit, atop the bathroom cabinet, and feels a pang of sadness for her lonely friend Michael. He is such a good man and deserves happiness just like anybody else. She feels like a bad friend for never having thought that he might be lonely and looking for someone special to share his life with.

When she returns to the living area, Michael is back in the kitchen boiling the kettle again.

She forces a smile.

'Thanks, Michael, I feel so much better now. I just need to own my mistake and do my best to move forward and make sure...' Her voice quavers. 'Make sure I'm a better person from now on. A better wife and a better mother and a better friend. Just a better all-round human being.'

Leni's face. Oh God. She'll never, for the life of her, forget Leni's face.

Samantha wonders, briefly, if sex is now ruined for her. She's always enjoyed sex and has been blessed – or perhaps cursed – with a high sex drive. But for the first time in her life, she sees sex as sordid and seedy, dirty and nasty and... there is nothing romantic about what she did with Nathan. Nothing beautiful about it at all. It had been ugly. Plain and simple.

She doesn't ever want to see him again. Doesn't want to have to look him in the eye. Maybe they'll have to move house. Start afresh.

Michael gives her a reassuring hug at the door, which she doesn't want to end, and sends her on her way.

Samantha walks quickly, the rapidly darkening sky, heavy with rainclouds, a blessing as she scurries away like the cockroach she feels she is, across Michael's immaculately mowed lawn, deliberately avoiding looking anywhere near the double-story house directly across the street, and especially the upstairs room Leni had discovered them in.

Grass crunches beneath her feet and somewhere distant thunder rumbles.

Tristan's light is on and Samantha's legs turn to water. She feels like dissolving again, just disappearing. She wonders if he knows already. Will he storm downstairs and have a go at her? Remind her of the despicable human that she is? He has every right to, Samantha thinks.

Of course Leni will have said something. They are best friends. They were the best of friends before they became a couple. They tell each other everything.

Leni will have told him straight away.

Samantha sucks in a deep breath and turns the doorknob and walks in.

Orlando must have cooked dinner because the smell of pizza fills her nostrils.

He greets her with a huge smile. A smile that rips her heart in two.

'Just frozen pizzas. I thought we could do with an easy night,' he says, his voice soft and kind.

Samantha's throat tightens, she wants to bawl but holds it in and walks right up to him and wraps her arms around him.

She wants to say 'I'm sorry' over and over again, but words won't budge from her throat.

'It's okay, love. I'm hungover too. The pizza will sort you out,' he says with a laugh.

Samantha's blood runs cold. Maybe he doesn't know? She's not sure what is better, Orlando knowing or not... but decides that either way, she feels hideous. She's a monster.

Tristan comes down the stairs, slowly, shuffling his feet and frowning. Each step that brings him closer to

Samantha terrifies her. She draws away from Orlando and hides her trembling hands behind the kitchen counter.

'Hey, buddy, are you okay?' asks Orlando, his eyes following Tristan. 'You get an entire pizza to yourself.'

'I'm not hungry.'

Samantha feels herself pale, literally feels the blood drain from her face.

'What's the matter?' she asks, her voice cracking as she readies herself for the onslaught of hateful words that she deserves.

'Leni,' says Tristan, meeting Samantha's eyes. Tristan and Samantha have always had a close relationship. A mummy's boy, Orlando often teased light-heartedly.

'She's not answering my texts.' He leans against the counter, looking down, his veiny hands making fists. 'And I think it's all my fault.'

'Of course it isn't your fault, love. Of course not,' she says, coming over to Tristan and rubbing his back, feeling like the fraud she is.

*It's my fault*, she thinks sadly.

All my fault.

# 22

## *Tristan*

Tristan stares hard at the kitchen floor tiles and tries to force away the tears that his tingling nose tells him are about to burst free.

Leni.

She won't respond to his messages and his stomach churns at the possibility that she doesn't want him around anymore.

Did he ask for too much too soon? Did he push her too far? And although they didn't actually do anything last night, he wonders if the overall pressure of him wanting it has pushed her away.

Maybe she never wants to see him again.

'You couldn't harm a fly, love. I'm sure it's nothing you've done. She's probably just busy,' says his mum.

It irritates Tristan that his issues with Leni are seen as 'nothing'.

'No,' he says, trying to keep his voice steady. 'She always responds. And it says she read the first message. The others just delivered. She knows I've written and she hasn't written back and she's not answering my calls. I feel like some kind of stalker now. Of my own girlfriend.'

His mum attempts to draw him into a hug but he steps away from her.

'You'll feel better after some pizza,' she says, sounding ridiculously upbeat, and acting as though eating food will solve all of his problems.

It annoys him to no end. He loves his mum, but he could almost say that she seems relieved to hear that Leni isn't responding to him. What's that all about?

His mum, and his dad for that matter, have been acting strange all day and it's left him wondering what on earth they'd gotten up to last night. With his mum acting weirdly depressed all day until now, and his dad being so overly upbeat and happy, *and* Leni not speaking to him, he has to wonder if something strange went down at Leni's parents' gatho last night. Something bad.

There was that fight between Alison and Rory, that the entire street will have heard, but that's not exactly something new or even a reason for all of this weirdness.

He allows his imagination to go crazy as he wonders what could have happened to cause Leni to stop talking to him. Maybe his mum told Leni's mum something about Tristan while she was drunk last night. Something that has turned Leni off.

He can't imagine what, but now paranoia is kicking in. It would explain things. Because, why on earth, after such an amazing night together, would Leni ignore his texts?

She's never left him on read, ever. Not even when they weren't dating.

His dad slips an entire pepperoni pizza onto a large white dinner plate and pours a glass of cola over ice for him.

'Come on, mate, by the time you eat that pizza and drink your drink, your phone will be blowing up with messages from Leni.'

Tristan sighs and plonks himself down at the dinner table, but as he glances up from his pepperoni pizza, he catches a look pass between his parents, a strange look loaded with… what? Tristan has never seen them look at each other in that way.

The skin along his arms prickle with goosebumps. Something is going on.

He takes a bite of pizza and chews, hardly tasting anything.

Something just doesn't add up.

Earlier in the day, he'd seen his father scrolling through Leni's mum's Facebook page, which is weird. His dad didn't know that Tristan was right behind him and had clicked on a bikini pic of Laura, which Tristan knows is old because it was from Leni's holiday in Broome last year.

But why on earth would his dad be stalking Leni's mum? Did his dad have a secret crush on Laura? And had his mum found out? Is this why they are behaving so weirdly?

He *has* to see Leni. Desperately needs to speak to her. Who knows? Maybe something is up between her parents. Shit, she might be having family problems and here he is, being a selfish, whiny prick just because she hasn't answered a few texts.

He knows what he has to do. He'll go to Leni's house and climb up the tree and knock on her window and surprise her. Then, once she sees him, she'll want him there for her. She'll want him to make everything better with one of his bear hugs, the kind she loves.

Yeah. That's it. Leni is going through family stuff. She hasn't stopped loving him. She isn't ignoring him. She's likely just hiding away in her bedroom trying to process some intense stuff on her own because she's like that. Leni is always trying to cushion people away from pain and hurt. She's so kind and it is one of the many reasons why it has been so easy to fall in love with her.

Tristan forces down a couple of slices of pizza and skols his Coke to keep his parents happy.

'Thanks.'

'Feel better now?' his dad asks.

Tristan fakes one of his winning smiles.

'Yeah, I do actually. I'm gonna go grab a shower.'

His mother smiles but it doesn't quite reach her eyes. In fact, her eyes look like black holes right now. A shiver travels down Tristan's spine as he tries to shake off the image of his mum looking like death. Something bad must have definitely happened last night. He is certain of it.

Glancing over his shoulder to make sure his parents aren't watching, he walks quickly down the corridor, bypasses the bathroom and leaves the house via the laundry door and heads straight out into the yard.

He lets himself out the side gate and crosses the lamplit street.

Soft light glows from Leni's room. Her curtains are drawn shut.

Tristan's heart starts working faster.

*Please, be a misunderstanding,* he thinks. *Or family problems.* Then he feels guilty for hoping it's that. He doesn't actually want his girlfriend to have family problems.

Or just let there be something wrong with Leni's phone. A bug or a glitch that they'll laugh about later while cuddling beneath her doona.

He raps his knuckles against her windowpane and waits, his breath held.

When around a minute passes, he does it again, this time a little louder.

The light in her room suddenly vanishes and he is left staring into darkness.

Tristan feels all the blood in his head drain to his feet.

Leni turning the light off is the biggest 'fuck off' he's ever received in his life and it hurts. It hurts so much because it's Leni.

The climb back down the tree is difficult. His legs tremble so badly that he slips and falls to the ground, jarring his ankles.

Fuck, fuck, fuck.

While he clutches at his feet, tears spring to his eyes.

Leni doesn't love him anymore.

Overnight, he has become someone that she does not want around.

This has to be the truth.

She simply doesn't want him anymore.

*The truth hurts,* he thinks, as he lies back on the wet grass, his ankles throbbing, the black sky swallowing him whole.

While the wet dew seeps into his shirt and pants, Tristan wonders what he's done.

What could possibly have caused Leni, his best friend and girlfriend, to want him out of her life so suddenly?

He wonders if she'll ever speak to him again.

And he wonders if he'll ever recover, or ever feel happiness again.

# 23

***Rory***

Rory replays the day's events over and over as he lies in bed beside his sleeping wife.

He feels so good. Hasn't felt this way in a long time. And yet it's strange, because none of this would have happened had the street not decided to host a key party, as weird as that sounds.

After last night's disaster, he'd taken the kids out for the evening and had driven them to their favourite spot at the beach for fish and chips. He'd taken a beer for himself so that he could think and take his time to decide what to do next with regards to his crumbling marriage.

Rory had taken his time with the kids at the beach, climbing the rocks with them and then throwing a few wish rocks into the sea. He'd even wished for his marriage to be saved as his rock had broken through the surface of the sea.

But after a while, after retreating back to the car to finish his beer and watch the kids climb up and down the rocks to search for baby crabs and jellyfish, the glaringly depressive state of his marriage to Alison had returned to worry away at his heart.

But just when he'd decided that this is it, that this is the time to give up, to let his marriage crumble and walk away, Alison had pulled up beside him in her own car, just as a soft rain had started to patter against his windows.

'You're very predictable,' she'd said, trying not to smile as she'd climbed into the passenger seat of his car.

Rory had recalled the words she'd screamed at him only hours before, about how much of a man Michael was and how she should just move out and shack up with him instead of Rory, because then at least the kids would have a man as a role model. A real man.

He'd tensed up, wanting to speak his mind, but not wishing things to escalate in front of the kids, who were running towards the car, grinning, after spying their mother.

'I'm sorry,' said Alison, tears in her eyes, her voice unusually soft. 'I'm really sorry, Rory. For everything. I've been an absolute monster.'

The kids had all gathered at Alison's window where, outside, rain still sprinkled.

'Can we climb the rocks again? In the rain?' their eldest asked, her blue eyes, so like Rory's, lit up with the prospect of rock-climbing in the rain.

Rory had looked at Alison, who normally threw a fit if the kids got wet because it meant soggy clothes and footprints throughout the house.

But this time she had smiled wide, even as the rain came down harder still.

'Of course you can, kids. Just be careful, please. The rocks will be extra slippery.'

The kids threw their hands up to the sky and raced towards the rocks.

Rory stared at this alien being pretending to be his wife.

'I'm so sorry, Rory. I've been a bitch. Not just last night, but... for the past year or so. I don't know what's gotten into me.' Tears had glazed her eyes then. 'I think it's work. I don't know. I just, come home and see you and I feel like you look so relaxed all the time with the kids, and they love you so much more than they do me.'

Rory shakes his head.

'No. They don't. They love you. They can't wait to see you when you get home. You just need to work on your moods. You can't bring the dramas of work home with you. We should be your safe haven.'

'I know... and I've decided to make a big change starting today.' She had looked into his eyes, tears pooling and spilling over her cheeks, and reached out to run her fingers along the back of his hand.

Rory had felt torn. On one hand, he hadn't been touched like this by Alison in so long, hadn't heard compassion in her voice in forever, and he'd missed it, he missed it so much. But at the same time, he still felt unsure, too scarred by all the hurtful things she'd said to him the past year or so.

'I know it's not going to be easy for you. I know you've gotten to a point where you have to guard yourself from getting hurt any more than you already have. But... all I can offer you is my willingness to try. Really try. Please, Rory, please give me one more chance?'

She'd pleaded at him with tears in her eyes. The mother of his children – how could he not give her a chance? Somewhere deep inside this woman was the girl he'd fallen in love with. And he didn't want to let her go just yet.

'Of course, I'll give you another chance, Alison,' he'd said, his voice hoarse as he'd wrapped his arms tightly around her and bent his head to bury it in her hair.

She'd smelt so good. Oh God, he'd missed touching her. Missed being this close.

'How about I drive the kids home, pop them in the bath, then get them ready for bed while you get us a chilled bottle of sauvignon blanc?'

Rory had kissed Alison on the forehead and smiled. He'd felt something warm bloom in his chest. He hadn't felt it in such a long time.

'Sounds like a plan, my love.'

Alison looked up at him and pressed her soft lips against his and then her body.

'Later,' she'd said, winking. 'Once the kids are in bed, we can take our wine and ourselves into the bedroom.'

Later *had* happened. It hadn't been a false promise.

She'd even unstripped to have complete naked sex which they hadn't done in years, but she still made him do it with his eyes closed. That's something he's not sure will ever change.

But it had been sex nonetheless and she'd been sweet afterwards and held him after they'd gotten dressed to go into the lounge room and have a late-night disaster film movie marathon.

Now, at this midnight hour, Rory stares at his wife's sleeping form and thinks that the hardness that has developed in her face over the past year has softened a little.

He reaches out and strokes a lock of her long blonde hair away from her face and sighs.

*Please*, he wills his sleeping wife, *please try.*

# 24

## *Laura*

I stand in the kitchen cradling a cup of steaming coffee while I watch the rising sun work its magic, casting golden rays across the yard, lighting up my vegetable patch and the crunchy green lawn the kids love playing cricket on.

Everything feels so much better and hopeful on the tail of a new dawn. Once everyone on the street returns to their routines of work, school and tending to their kids and their mountain of other responsibilities, the disastrous weekend will sit where it belongs, in the past, and will eventually be forgotten.

Hopefully.

I set my coffee down and take out a loaf of sliced bread and the black pepper grinder from the pantry, some margarine, ham and lettuce from the fridge, before whipping together three ham sandwiches. There are only two apples in the fruit bowl and one banana. The boys and Leni are all going through a phase of hating bananas but I give it to Leni because she hates the offending yellow fruit the least out of the three.

When I search the pantry for snacks to put with the kids' lunches and find none, I sigh and resign myself to the fact that I'll have to brave the shops today, possibly during my lunchbreak, to stock up on all the bits and bobs we need to survive the week.

I wonder if I'll have time to buy a couple of takeaway coffees after the school drop-off this morning, before work. I could drop a flat white over to Rory and see how he's holding up after that train wreck of a weekend. Geez, the next suburb would have been able to hear Alison's screaming and shouting in the street on Saturday night.

My coffee's gone cold so I tip it down the sink and rinse out my mug, my thoughts straying to Rory and Naomi. They had looked so cosy and kind of cute before I'd burst in on them in the yard, bawling my eyes out like a baby. But then my head fills with the sounds of Nathan and Samantha's giggles from upstairs and I shake my head, put away the bread and the rest of the lunch things, and head upstairs to get the kids out of bed.

I'll have to try to shove everything from Saturday night in the darkest corner of my brain and just focus on the kids.

I wake the boys first, burying my face into their warm curls.

When I get to Leni's room, I knock first. But when I don't get the usual grumbling response that she's awake, I open the door to find my daughter's bed neatly made up.

Feeling slightly alarmed, I take my phone out of my dressing gown pocket and send Leni a quick 'where are you?' text before I dial Nathan, who is already at work. He answers on the third ring.

'Did you see Leni this morning?'

'No. Why?'

'She's not in bed – I don't even know if she slept in it. She didn't come down to dinner, remember? And I was so tired I fell asleep just after eight.'

An awful creepy feeling crawls up my neck and I shiver. What kind of a mother am I that I don't even know where my own daughter is, or if she even spent the night at home last night?

'Well, I checked in on her before I went to bed and she was in her room,' says Nathan.

'Did she seem okay?'

I can practically see Nathan shrugging on the other side of the phone. He probably has a million and one things to do at his worksite.

'I don't know. She yelled at me to get out when I started singing the *Giggle and Hoot* lullaby, but she always does that whenever I sing it. It's our little routine.' He chuckles.

'But did she say it in a jokey way, like she always does, or in a serious way?'

'Shit, love, I've got to go. Contractors are here. Look, she's probably gone along with Tristan to an early morning surf. They said on the radio that the conditions are perfect today. I wouldn't be surprised.'

Another sigh of relief. Of course. Tristan. Wherever Tristan is, I'm sure to find Leni. I smile and inwardly brand myself silly for assuming the worst. It's a habit I'd formed since the tender age of eight, while in primary school, after one of my favourite teachers, Miss Kingston, had died suddenly in a car accident. Ever since, I have always expected the worst.

My mum and dad used to have a bit of a laugh about it. If we were expecting visitors and they were no more than ten minutes late I'd apparently stare out the living room window and dramatically announce to all in the room that sadly, our visitors must have died in a car accident.

'Okay, I really have to go. Bye,' says Nathan.

'Okay, thanks...' I am about to say 'love' but then remember that I'm still upset with him for following Samantha up our stairs so enthusiastically on Saturday night. 'See you tonight,' I say coolly.

'Okay. See you then.'

Before I have a chance to end the call, he clears his throat and says, 'Laura?'

'Yeah?'

'I love you.'

I pause and think about asking what exactly he'd done with Samantha, but then I recall the rules Alison had read out. No discussing what happened afterwards. There is an obvious reason behind that rule and in that split second, I decide to respect it. More so to protect me than Nathan.

'I know you do,' I say, my voice cracking. 'I do too,' I add, because it's true no matter what.

The boys have emerged from their bedrooms, messy-haired and sleepy-eyed. Both come at me from either side and wrap their warm thin little arms around my waist. Their morning ritual. Normally I giggle and tickle them both beneath their chins, but my mind is still on Leni and her un-creased, perfectly made bed. Though I know that Nathan's suggestion of Leni being with Tristan is very likely, I'm still mildly concerned at Leni's headspace seeing as some of our friends were still at our house on Saturday night when she returned from Tristan's and I'm worried she saw something she shouldn't have.

'Where's Leni?' asks Austin, who has followed my gaze into his sister's bedroom.

'She's with Tristan,' I say, reaching into my dressing gown pocket to check if Leni has read her message. But it is still sitting on delivered. 'But I'm sure you'll see her today after school,' I add, my heart now flapping about anxiously in my chest. What if Leni fails to return home this afternoon? Or tonight?

'I'm hungry,' says Billy.

'Well, how about I make you both an egg on toast and a strawberry smoothie?'

'Yay.'

'Yum!' says Austin, happily following his little brother down the stairs. He pauses, mid-step and glances up at me, his dark brown eyes round with something akin to fear.

'Um... I may have forgotten to do an assignment this weekend.'

'When's it due?'

'Today,' he says, his face dropping.

I groan inwardly. The last thing I feel like doing this morning, while Leni is God-knows-where, is throwing together a haphazard assignment for my forgetful son. But of course I'll help him. Thank God for my late-start Monday mornings. I'll have to skip coffee with Rory though. Perhaps I'll send Nathan around to see him after work with a couple of beers. Nathan certainly owes me a few favours after encouraging Saturday night to happen.

'Well, how about I make brekky while you get your things out ready for working on the assignment.' I ruffle his bed hair. 'I'll help. We'll do it in no time. We've done this before, remember? Don't look so glum.'

'Yeah, but I only got 50% last time we did it like this.'

'Better than zero,' I say, shrugging before entering the kitchen and putting breakfast on for my boys.

While I watch the eggs gently sizzle in olive oil, the toast pops up, startling me out of my thoughts which of course were of Leni and Nathan and Saturday night.

After I butter the toast, I check my phone again. Leni still hasn't read her message. My heart beats a little faster. Leni is always, without question, glued to her phone. So why isn't she checking her messages?

I risk leaving the eggs unattended and race upstairs to check for Leni's schoolbag and see that it's gone. Which is a good thing. If something extreme had occurred then Leni would hardly have taken the time to take her schoolbag along with her.

I decide that if I haven't heard from Leni by school drop-off time, then I'll text Tristan. I don't know why I'm not messaging him already. Perhaps it's because I don't want to know. My mother's intuition tells me that something is wrong. That Leni isn't with her boyfriend. She is too responsible a daughter for her to have casually left the house with Tristan without telling me about it. We've always had a great relationship, and share an extra special mother-daughter bond, an unbreakable bond I've always thought.

But here I am, unsure where my teenage daughter is, and even worse, unsure if my daughter even slept in the house last night.

After the boys scoff their eggs and get dressed, I sit down with Austin and help him to write the best Italian comic book story about animals that we can think up on the fly.

Only twenty minutes later, I'm in the car in the driveway, the boys buckled in their seats in the back. Before I put the car in reverse, I tap out a quick text to Tristan.

*Hi Tristan,*
*Is Leni with you? If she is can you please ask her to message me?*
*Thanks love!*
*Laura :-)*

The text is read almost immediately, which sets off alarm bells in my mind.

*She's not. She hasn't responded to any of my messages since late Sat night.*
*I'm worried. :-(*

Then, after a few seconds, he sends this:

*Did she say anything at all about me? Or did she seem upset on Saturday night? I think I may have upset her.*

*I'm sorry.*

'Mum, we're going to be late for school,' both my boys say in unison.

'Where's Leni?'

'Shush, boys, we're not late. Leni's with... Tristan, remember?' I lie.

I quickly reply to Tristan's text, feeling bad for hoping that Leni and Tristan have had a fight and that my daughter has just gone to school early to avoid him.

'Did you two have a fight?' I text.

> *No... but... I don't know how to say this.*
> *I may have scared her away.*
> *I don't know.*
> *Sorry.*

I'm not quite sure what to say to that. Tristan is such a sweet and gentle boy. Maybe the two of them have simply moved too fast.

> *Let's talk later, after school. Can you please text me if you see her at school? Don't force her if she doesn't want to talk. Just let me know that she's safe.*

> *Okay. Sure thing. Thanks, Laura.*

> *No. Thank you, Tristan.*
> *Everything will be okay by the end of the day, I'm sure of it :-)*

> *I hope so :-(*

I drop the boys at the drop-and-kiss line, instead of walking them in like I usually do. They are beyond excited at the prospect of being 'like the other kids' who get to be dropped off drive-by style every day.

As I watch them happily skip away from the car, tears sting my eyes. Austin turns and gives me a thumbs up and mouths 'thank you' waving the assignment in the air. Billy gives me two thumbs up.

God, I love my kids. I would die for them. I truly would.

Now, I need to find Leni and work out what the heck is going on.

My phone pings minutes later, just as I'm crawling, curbside in my car, by my daughter's high school, in hopes of seeing her.

It's Leni.

I indicate left and pull the car into the nearest parking bay.

> *Hey Mum, sorry. I realised I've got a test today and so met some friends at Maccas to study over brekky. Sorry I forgot to tell you xx*

I read and re-read the text, searching for vital clues. It isn't right. Leni just does not leave the house to meet with friends so early in the morning without telling me about it in advance. Plus, usually if she does anything like this it's with Tristan. Not that I'm unhappy about her meeting with friends. I'm actually very happy about that... if it's true. Because no good can come from depending on one person entirely, and as much as I love Tristan, they could both do with a bit of balance in their lives.

I breathe a sigh of relief. At least I've heard from her. At least I know she's alive and well enough to text.

> *Okay, no probs. Best of luck on your test and let's have a nice chat tonight over a cup of that tea you like :-) xx*

Leni texts back a kissy face and two 'x's and I feel a little better about everything. Maybe everything is going to be okay. Maybe nothing is wrong and I'm overthinking things as usual.

I tap back a quick 'Love you Leni'.

Intending on going in early to work, I put on my indicator, but fail to pull out of the carpark before my phone pings with a text. And then another.

The first one is from Orlando.

> *Can we meet at the cafe? Or the beach? Please? I need to tell you something important.*

I contemplate ignoring him but the last thing I need is him coming over to my house with Samantha one day and things getting awkward between us. I'll just have to hear him out, whatever it is he needs to get off his chest, then get on with my day.

> *Okay, I'll be at the cafe in five. I only have a couple minutes though. We can chat in carpark.*

The next is from Tristan.

> *Leni's not at school. I asked her friends and none of them have seen or heard from her.*

My heart sinks. I immediately call work and tell them I have a family emergency and that I'm terribly sorry but I can't come in. Not ideal when you're a new employee, but I need to find my daughter first and to find out if she's okay.

I contemplate cancelling on Orlando, but instincts tell me that what he has to say is indeed important. Perhaps it's to do with Leni. Plus, it's only five minutes of my time.

A cloud moves and covers the golden, morning sun with its bleakness.

It is then that I know something is very wrong.

# 25

## *Samantha*

Samantha puts her phone down and sighs with temporary relief. She had to call in sick at work. She can't face being looked at – even though nobody there would have the faintest idea of what she'd done over the weekend. She feels as though she's wearing a big neon sign above her head flashing 'Adulterer' in red lights. Crossing the front lawn to the mailbox felt bad enough. She'd had to wait until the postie had driven off as she hadn't even wanted to face him – a practical stranger.

She'd given Tristan a big hug that morning before he'd left for school and had noticed a redness to his eyes. The kid hasn't cried since he was eleven and her heart aches for him and his situation right now.

She thinks of Leni and can't get the sight of the girl's face, the way that her skin had paled and her eyes had widened when she'd seen Nathan and her half-naked on the floor, out of her head.

Oh God.

Samantha's face floods with heat. She will never get over this. No amount of time can heal this – that is, unless she can go back in time. That is the only possible way she can fix this mess.

She puts the kettle on and starts sifting through the mail when she notices a handwritten, non-addressed envelope with her name scrawled across it in red pen. With trembling fingers, she tears it open.

The kettle whistles, but Samantha ignores it.

A torn piece of paper, half the size of an A4 sheet, has been stuffed inside the envelope.

Samantha's breath becomes trapped in her throat, and her heart stops when she sees what has been scrawled across the piece of paper.

*Fucking slut!*

She stares at the handwriting and though it appears slanted and masculine – an obvious attempt at disguising the author's handwriting, she knows who's written it. Leni, of course. It has to be.

And Samantha can't blame her.

How can she? That poor girl has witnessed another woman fucking her father. Her boyfriend's mother no less.

Samantha closes her eyes as flashbacks assault her mind. She'd been so drunk that she hadn't noticed Leni in the room at first, hadn't even noticed that it had been Leni's room that they'd fallen into. Nathan had seemed oblivious to his environment also. Samantha recalls groaning out loud and grinding her hips… all while Leni had been watching.

Oh God.

She wants to die. Dying is the only solution, the only way out of this mess.

She picks up her phone and starts tapping out a text to Tristan, asking him to please apologise to Leni for what she saw Saturday night, but then Samantha remembers that Leni isn't responding to Tristan's texts.

And it's all Samantha's fault.

Leni is obviously upset and disgusted by what she saw and she doesn't know how to tell Tristan. Doesn't know how to tell her boyfriend that his mum and her dad had betrayed them all.

Poor Tristan. And Poor Leni. How could Samantha and Nathan have done something so stupid? How could they have made a young girl take on such a weighty responsibility?

Samantha knows what she needs to do.

She takes a bottle of vodka out of the freezer and takes a long drag. She needs it to settle her nerves. She is going to have to keep busy today, pottering around the house in order to pass the time until after 3pm. And then, when Tristan comes home, she'll tell him what happened on Saturday night. It is the only way.

Honesty, even if it hurts, is the only way.

It is a phrase she'd taught Tristan his whole life and he's always been honest to a fault, even as a little kid.

Samantha wonders if Orlando actually knows that she slept with Nathan. She has no way of knowing what he knows or what he thinks about it because they have both been respecting Alison's rules.

No. He must know, she thinks. He's been acting strangely since Sunday morning. Whenever Samantha suggests they should talk, he brushes her off and either cracks a joke or behaves extra lovingly towards her. It's strange. Almost like he's trying to pretend that Saturday night never happened.

He knows. And he still wants to be with me.

Samantha's head throbs with confusion and self-disgust.

I must call Laura.

Orlando may be trying to avoid confrontation, but Samantha needs to address it somehow. She needs to tell somebody other than Michael that it had all been a terrible mistake.

Samantha grabs her phone and heads out the front door, braving the outdoors and the potential judgement from any neighbours who are home. She crosses the street to Laura's, finger-combing her hair while she walks. The air is crisp, fresh and she rubs at her bare arms as she crosses Laura and Nathan's crunchy front lawn.

'Samantha!'

Samantha freezes in her tracks and slowly turns around.

Naomi is standing across the street, a beach towel over her shoulder and her hair damp from her usual morning swim and walk. Something she's always done as part of her daily routine – no matter what the weather.

Naomi will be starting work soon and as such Samantha knows that her friend won't hang around for too long. She won't ask too many questions either – Naomi is far from nosey. Samantha doesn't know if it is because Naomi is polite or if she just has a way of reading people without needing to ask any questions.

'Hey,' says Samantha, her phone almost slipping from her sweaty grasp. She grips it tighter and glances at Laura's house and wonders now if she is even home. She knows that Laura starts later on Mondays... but right now, Samantha suddenly doesn't feel quite as ready to face Laura as she had felt a minute ago.

Her stomach churns as Naomi approaches her and puts a cool hand on her arm.

'Hey. Are you okay?' Naomi asks, her dark brown eyes filled with concern.

Samantha feels her chin quiver. It hasn't quivered like that since she was a little girl. She isn't the kind of woman who cries at the drop of a hat. She's never been that way. When all the other mums quietly cry in the darkness of the cinema during the latest Disney film, Samantha is usually the one eyerolling. But today, under the concerned gaze of her friend Naomi, she feels like bawling like a five-year-old.

'No,' says Samantha, after some time. She swallows down the tears that threaten to spill and starts to take a step back, towards her house.

'Look, if you've got ten minutes, come to mine,' says Naomi. 'You look like you could do with a nice strong coffee. I'll give you my special two-sugars espresso,' Naomi says, raising her brows and smiling.

Samantha allows herself to be led by Naomi, who tugs at her gently, until she finds herself sitting on a couch inside her neighbour's beautiful family home.

'You know what, I'm so proud of you,' says Samantha suddenly.

'You've achieved so much and you're a single mum, a widower, bringing up three kids all by yourself while still working fulltime as a grief counsellor. You're my hero, you know.' She clears her throat and feels tears threaten.

Oh God. No. No. No.

She sucks in a fortifying breath and smiles. 'And you're an angel too. Always so kind. Such a good soul.'

Unlike me, thinks Samantha. I'm the bitch who sleeps behind my husband's back.

And before she can stop herself, she bursts into tears right there on the couch.

'Hey, you're pretty amazing too,' says Naomi, over the sound of the coffee machine. 'Tristan is one of the most kind-hearted and remarkably sensible teenage boys I've ever met. He's wonderful. Intelligent and sweet. He's a credit to you, you know. To both you and Orlando.'

Within seconds Naomi is sitting right beside Samantha and rubbing her back, which only serves to make Samantha cry harder.

'I slept with Nathan. And Leni came in and saw us. I haven't even spoken to Laura about it. I'm not even sure that she knows,' Samantha splutters out between sobs. 'I don't know what to do. I've messed up, Naomi. I've messed up big time and I don't know how to fix it.' She meets Naomi's eyes. 'I want to die. I really do.' She pauses, then realised that what she's said is insensitive to Naomi's situation.

'Oh, you poor love,' says Naomi soothingly, rubbing Samantha's back in soft circles.

'Oh gosh, there I go again. Being selfish. Poor David didn't have a say, did he? And here I am being a whiny bitch wishing I were dead. I'm so sorry. I'm sorry Naomi.' She gets to her feet and starts rushing down the hallway to the front door. 'I've got to go.'

Ignoring Naomi's pleas to come back, she runs out the front door, past Laura's, and instead of going home, goes straight to Michael's place.

Normally he'd be at work but his ute is sitting in the carport. He didn't seem hungover yesterday, but sometimes he has a few too many drinks when he is feeling particularly lonely, *'to drown my lonely sorrows'* he'd once told Samantha.

She knocks on the door, but when Michael doesn't answer, she finds it unlocked and lets herself in.

Samantha wrinkles her nose at the smell of vomit and something else bad and immediately regrets not slipping some shoes on before leaving the house earlier. Glass crunches beneath her bare soles and the sting of something sharp slicing into her foot makes her swear.

She gasps. There is blood all over the floor. Not just hers. Somebody else's. Dried blood. Sticky blood.

'Michael?' she calls.

No answer.

She leans against the wall with one hand while she digs out the offending piece of bloodstained glass and brushes away the other tiny shards on each foot before stepping over the mess, which appears to have once been a bottle of some kind of whiskey or bourbon. She makes her way, cautiously, into the kitchen, her breath held, her pulse deafening in her ears.

'Michael?' she calls, her heart hammering against her ribcage.

Nothing. A breeze stirs the curtains from an open window and Naomi shivers. She hopes that nothing bad has happened. She simply cannot bear the thought of anything bad happening to Michael. Not her best friend.

She checks his bedroom first and finds the crumpled sheets of an unmade bed and several empty beer bottles resting on the floor.

So, he's had one of his benders. She wonders what has sent him over the edge and prays that it isn't anything to do with Saturday night. She feels like a terrible friend. She should have asked him yesterday. For all Samantha knew, Michael might also have been feeling pretty shitty about something he'd done.

Panicking now, she searches the other rooms, then the bathroom. But he isn't inside the house at all.

She checks the kitchen for some kind of note but finds none.

But her breath catches in her throat when she spies a red pen and a torn piece of paper – roughly the same size as the one that had been placed in that envelope in her mailbox. The same piece of paper that somebody had written 'Fucking Slut!' on, in red pen.

Samantha becomes unsteady on her feet.

*Michael* sent the note? Her best friend? Had what she'd done with Nathan affected him this badly? But he seemed so normal yesterday and had been so kind towards Samantha.

This doesn't make any sense.

Samantha shivers as a cold chill creeps up her back. She stumbles out of the house, unsure of what to do next. She isn't sure who she should turn to about this.

She glances at Michael's ute as she walks up the driveway and notices that the driver's door is ajar.

That's odd, she thinks. Michael always makes fun of people who are stupid enough to let their car batteries run flat like this.

She sighs and decides to shut it for him, but stifles a scream when she spies him sitting there, in the driver's seat, head dangling back and eyes closed.

Dried blood covers his hands.

Sam tries to speak but a silent scream remains trapped inside her throat.

Michael makes a sound in his throat and she realises, with great relief, that he has been sleeping all along.

She exhales, finally, as she watches his sleeping form.

He's likely had too much to drink and passed out cold in his car before he got to drive.

*Thank God,* she thinks. *Thank God* he's okay.

Something buzzes on his lap and she sees a pink phone vibrate to life against his thigh.

Sam steps a little closer to inspect this pink phone that most certainly does not belong to Michael.

The message is from 'Tristan'.

*I love you.*

There is another message.

It's from 'Mum' with a ladybird emoji beside it and it reads, 'Love you, Leni.'

Sam feels bile rise up in her throat. Her head pounds in confusion.

The phone is bloody, just like Michael's hands.

It belongs to Leni.

Tristan hasn't heard from Leni since Saturday night.

What on earth is Michael doing with Leni's phone?

Oh God, she thinks. Oh God.

Sam runs, stumbling, towards Laura's house, all the while thinking, *what have you done, Michael, what have we all done?*

# 26

## *Orlando*

'Thanks for coming,' says Orlando. 'I've already ordered your almond milk latte because I know you've got work.'

'Oh, okay. Thanks.'

Laura fiddles with a loose strand of her hair and Orlando can see that she is visibly uncomfortable in his company.

He starts to second-guess his reasons for asking her to meet up with him.

What on earth had he been thinking this morning?

His face flushes at the memory.

To think that he was actually going to confront Laura with what he believes went on between Sam and Nathan and ask if she'd like to even everything up by meeting in a hotel room one night to have sex?

He shakes his head and rubs the back of his neck after they sit down in the farthest little booth in the cafe, the one that doesn't give them much of a view of the ocean, but at least gives them some privacy.

'Are you okay?' asks Laura, concern filling her hazel eyes.

Orlando's heart melts. *I do have a crush*, he thinks. Oh shit. *What the hell is going on?*

But it's Sam that he wants. And although she hasn't mentioned one word about Nathan or what they got up to on Saturday night, Orlando knows that he's lost her. She puts on a fake smile whenever Tristan is around, but once their son is gone, she's like an empty shell, staring out the window for hours. No eye contact.

Orlando feels sick whenever he thinks about his mate and his wife sleeping together. He wonders how he'll actually react if it is proven to be true.

Bile rises up his throat.

The coffees arrive in takeaway cups just like he'd asked, so they can leave and drink them on the run should they need to.

He looks at Laura, at her dishevelled appearance, which is unlike her, and his blood runs cold.

It must be true. Nathan must have confessed to her last night. Because why else would Laura look such a mess?

'Are you okay, Laura?' Orlando asks. 'You look like you've seen a ghost.'

Laura takes a sip of her coffee, her eyes staring into space. She blinks and finally meets Orlando's eyes.

'It's Leni,' she says, sighing deeply. 'She left early today and I didn't know where she'd gone. Felt like a bad mother, to be honest.' A pink blush warms Laura's cheeks. 'I had to text Tristan to see if she was with him.'

'Was she?' Orlando frowns. He knows she couldn't have been because Tristan was at home that morning and left the usual time to go to school. He did look distressed though and was on his phone the entire time. Orlando wonders if Tristan knows something about Sam and Nathan, because he's been acting strangely since Saturday night.

'No,' says Laura, her face white again. 'She texted me to say that she met with friends to study before a test, but Tristan told me that she didn't even show up to school.' Laura shrugs, but her eyes redden and shine with unshed tears. 'I don't even know where my own daughter is.'

Orlando isn't sure what to say. He thinks that maybe Leni knows something about Saturday night. Possibly Tristan knows too. He thinks his marriage is potentially over and that Sam and Nathan are going to carry on some kind of secret affair, and he feels like his life as he knew it, as a happily married man, is over.

'What is it?' Laura asks. 'If you know something about Leni, please tell me.'

Orlando feels his heart race. He doesn't want to stress Laura out any more than she already is. But he can't help himself. Plus, it might help Laura with Leni.

'I think Sam and Nathan may have done something together. On Saturday night.'

Laura takes a few seconds to process this. Takes a sip of her coffee and swallows before meeting Orlando's gaze.

'How do you know?'

Orlando can visibly see the hurt in Laura's eyes.

'I don't. I just know that Sam is acting strange and that Tristan hasn't been the same. I think he may have had an argument or something with Leni. All I know is that she hasn't been answering his texts back since Saturday night.'

'Really?'

Orlando looks at Laura and his face flushes with shame for having even contemplated asking this woman for sex. She's the mother of his son's girlfriend, she's the wife of his best mate. She's a friend.

A wave of disgust swirls inside his stomach. He stands.

'Sorry for calling you here, Laura. I know you have work, and...' He looks at his phone. 'I've got a meeting with a client I'm going to miss if I don't leave now.'

He reaches over and takes her hand. 'You're a good friend, Laura. Tristan loves you and so does Sam. Thanks for being there for them.'

Laura's hand drops away as soon as he lets go, as though she's too weak to hang on. She looks so tired, and thin and vulnerable that he's suddenly angry at himself, at Nathan, at Alison. Why were they all so stupidly excited by the idea of sleeping around with each other, with their friends?

He thinks about his non-stop fantasies of Laura that have plagued him since Saturday night, and as he watches her walk out of the cafe, looking distressed and heartbroken at the same time, he prays that this is the end of them. That this is where he stops being a horny immature boy and starts to be a responsible man who looks out for his family and friends.

He glances down at his phone. He wants to call Sam but decides to attend to the meeting first. But after that, it's time to have a good talk with his wife. And then maybe they can put all of this behind them and move forward.

# 27

## *Laura*

I jump at the sound of intrusive rapping at my front door and my heart panics. Whoever's at the front door is not Leni. Because Leni doesn't knock. She has her own set of keys.

So, it's either good news or bad news.

My stomach swirls, and my mouth grows dry as I head to the front door.

The door-pounding continues. I stop and peek out the lounge room window before I answer it, to check for the dreaded sight of a police van, but find no cars in my driveway apart from my own.

I breathe a small sigh of relief and tell myself that I'm being silly, that Leni is okay, that she probably just needs some space like Nathan suggested.

After running a hand through my hair and composing myself, I finally answer the door.

'Sam?' I say, when I see a trembling, pale woman that resembles my vibrant, strong friend standing at my door. 'Oh, my goodness, what happened to you?'

My gaze is drawn down to Sam's left foot, which appears to be bleeding. 'Come in so I can take a look at that. Is it deep?'

Sam covers her face with her hands and remains rooted to the front doormat.

'Did you see Leni this morning?' she asks through the gaps between her fingers. 'You need to tell me if you've seen her,' she says, coming off the mat to grip me firmly by the shoulders.

My insides plunge to my feet and my heart stops. I shake her hands off me.

'What do you mean? Did something happen to Leni?'

When Sam says nothing, I seize her by the shoulders and shake her a little.

'Did something happen to her?'

Tears slide down Sam's red cheeks.

'So, you haven't seen her?' asks Sam between sobs.

I stare at her. Sam crying. Sam bleeding, Sam knowing something about Leni being missing.

'Oh God,' says Sam. 'Oh God, Laura. I think something's happened to her. Something bad.' Sam stumbles away from the door and out into the front garden and proceeds to vomit onto my succulent plants.

'What? What do you mean?'

The world around me spins.

I step out the front door and grip Sam by her shoulders again, this time almost violently.

'What happened to Leni? Tell me!'

'Michael's... Leni's phone... oh God. The blood. There's blood everywhere. I'm sorry.' More tears stream down Sam's face. She wipes her eyes and the vomit from her chin. 'I'm so sorry, Laura, because I think it's all my fault.'

I leave Sam and race across the street to Michael's house, screaming my daughter's name, my pulse thundering in my ears.

'Leni! Leni!'

I bang on his front door and it opens wide, nobody inside but I can see dried blood mixed in with fresh blood, among shards of broken glass. 'Leni? Leni?'

'Laura?'

I spin around and see Michael leaning against his ute, rubbing his head and looking like he's just woken up. Confusion crinkles his face up.

My gaze falls on the dried blood all over his hands and my heart stops when I see Leni's pink phone within his bloody grasp.

The last thing I see is the pavement rising to smack me in the face.

# 28

### *Alison*

Alison wipes the steam away from the bathroom mirror with the palm of her hand so that she can better see her face.

Water drips down her back, between her breasts, along her legs and onto the bathmat while she critically appraises her appearance.

When she is like this, her skin stripped of makeup, her hair wet and untamed, her father's voice seems to rise up from the grave like a ghost on a mission.

'Ugly bitch.'

She stares at herself and nods.

'You're right, Dad. You're absolutely right,' she whispers, her eyes shiny with unshed tears, before she begins pinching at her scarred cheeks so hard that her face turns red and blotchy.

'Ugly dog,' she taunts her reflection. 'You're a waste of space. That's what you are. Can't even keep your husband happy. Even after all that surgery and all of that crap you've done to yourself. He doesn't want you anymore. He doesn't even love you. It's in his eyes. The spark's gone.'

She feels warm tears spill over her cheeks.

'No, no,' she whispers, her voice soft now. 'He wants me. He told me that he loves me. Rory loves me.'

A light rapping at the bathroom door causes Alison to jump. It frightens her dad's ghost away and sends him spinning back to his grave.

She clears her throat.

'Yes?'

'Allie, love. I've just had a call from Nathan. Laura's in hospital. She's had a fall and broke her nose. She fainted, according to Nathan.'

'What? Oh my God!' Alison unlocks the door.

Rory's eyes widen slightly. She knows this is because he hasn't seen her bare-faced, ever, not even before they married. She has simply never allowed it. Not even after fifteen years of marriage.

Luckily, Rory is kind enough to not comment.

'What happened?' she asks as she brushes past him and enters their walk-in robe to quickly find a pair of jeans and a clean shirt.

'She was in Michael's driveway. The police are there now, questioning him. This is what Nathan told me but... I don't know much... but they reckon he's had something to do with Leni's disappearance.'

Alison shoves her legs into her high-waisted jeans and quickly tugs her shirt on. She does the buttons up and emerges, dressed.

'What do you mean Leni's disappearance?'

Rory sucks in a deep breath and scratches the back of his head.

'She's gone missing. They think since Sunday night.'

'What?' She puts a hand to her lips.

'I know,' says Rory, shaking his head, his long hair momentarily covering his eyes. He flicks his fringe aside and meets her eyes. 'I don't know what to think. Michael's always been a good bloke.'

'What do you mean? Do they think he did something?'

'Potentially, yes. According to Nathan, Sam's blown away by it all. With Michael being her best friend, she doesn't know what to believe.' Rory sighs. 'When I saw her yesterday arvo, I must admit she looked pretty terrible. I think the weekend was hard on her.'

Alison nods and slips on some red flats. She feels responsible. If she hadn't gone half-mad and created that list of rules for the key party, like some kind of possessed freak, perhaps none of this would have happened. Perhaps nobody would have ever mentioned it again. It *is* her fault.

She leaves the room, Rory following close behind, and grabs the car keys.

Rory stares at her like she's lost her mind.

'You haven't... you haven't done your face,' he says, his voice hoarse, his eyes shiny with emotion.

'That doesn't matter. Laura is a friend and she needs me. I'm going to the hospital.'

'Okay. Well, you look beautiful,' Rory says. He stares at her for a very long time and then draws her into his arms.

She softens her rigid body and allows herself to sink into his embrace for a few moments. It feels nice. Good.

'Drive safe and... just be careful please.' He strokes her hair and draws back, gazing deep into her eyes. 'I need you. I think we need each other. The whole street... we all need to support each other through this... whatever this is.'

From the other room, Alison can hear the kids singing along with their favourite ABC program, and the beauty and innocence of their voices squeezes at her heart. She feels awful for how she's been behaving for the past couple of years. Ever since her dad passed away, she hasn't felt right. It's like it's brought him closer to her. The fact that he's a ghost now allows him to invade her life and haunt her every move.

Her thoughts return to Laura. How must she be feeling right now? Leni missing? Alison can't believe it. She refuses to believe it.

'Do they know what exactly happened to Leni?' asks Alison.

Rory shakes his head as they both enter the garage via the kitchen door. He hits the remote and the electronic roller door begins to rise up to reveal the dusky, dark grey sky. It still groans and creaks. He must look at it soon.

'No. But they found Michael with her phone. There was blood all over it.'

'What?' Alison pauses in shock for a moment before she climbs into her car. 'That sick fuck. I've always found him creepy.'

She tosses her handbag onto the passenger seat and leans out the window, shivering at the memory of the hand-job she'd given Michael on Saturday night.

'Tell the kids I love them and that I'll be back in an hour or so.' She shakes her head and swears. 'I can't believe this. Honestly. I just can't. It's like a bad dream.'

Alison turns the key in the ignition and starts the car. The engine hums loudly in the confines of the double garage.

Rory nods slowly as he steps away from the car.

Alison watches as one of her kids, their youngest girl, Sal, comes out and clings to Rory's leg, and Alison feels ridiculous for the pangs of jealousy that rise within her. Little-girl-Alison would have loved to have had a dad as loving and attentive as Rory.

Alison shakes her head and forces thoughts of her dad, which have come creeping up again, away.

She waves at Rory and Sal after she reverses out of the driveway, her stomach turning at the sight of the police wagon parked in Michael's driveway.

Twenty minutes later, she arrives at the hospital, parks and heads straight for the front desk.

'Laura Standoll, please.'

The woman gives her Laura's room number and Alison finds the nearest elevator. Once she arrives at the third floor, she makes her way down a wide, beige corridor, her stomach a swirling sea while everybody she passes makes no secret of staring at her, especially the little kids.

'Mummy, what's wrong with that lady's face?'

Alison spies a disabled toilet and quickly enters it, locking the heavy door behind her.

She stands in front of the small, rectangular mirror and gasps. The magnitude of seeing her bare face, raw with scars old and new, in the mirror of a public toilet takes her breath away. Why had she not put on makeup? How could she have thought that it would be okay to just go out without any makeup and allow the world to see her true self.

She slaps her scarred cheeks, making the pearly white lines on either side of her face stand out against the redness of her skin. She can feel her dead father standing behind her, his ghostly breath making her tremble.

'Ugly bitch.'

She is about to pinch the skin of her cheeks, hard, but something stops her.

Go away, Dad.

She's getting stronger lately. Able to tell her dad to back off. It doesn't work all the time but it's something. It's progress. She draws her shoulders back and stares deep into her eyes.

'You're here for Laura. You're here for your friend. Not to have people admire your artfully applied makeup.'

She glares at the space over her shoulder and mentally pictures her father standing there, smirking. She shakes him free from her mind.

'Fuck off,' she says. 'Fuck off and leave me alone.'

His presence is always the strongest on the anniversary of his death, which is coming in a few weeks. After the anniversary, Alison will feel stronger and hopefully this time he'll fade away for good, with Rory by her side.

She exits the bathroom and with her head held high, locates Laura's room and knocks on the open door.

'Hello?'

She pokes her head through and her breath catches when she spies Laura in bed, resting against a mountain of pillows, her nose bandaged and purplish bruises spreading outwards across her cheeks and beneath her eyes.

'Hey,' says Nathan, who immediately rises from his chair. 'Alison,' he says, staring at her. She can read the shock in his eyes, the shock at her appearance and maybe even the shock of her coming to the hospital to see Laura.

Nathan reaches for Laura's hand and gives it a squeeze. 'Look, love, it's Allie.'

Laura blinks and smiles for a millisecond before closing her eyes again.

The two boys, Austin and Billy, glance up from their Uno game spread out between them on the green carpet.

'Mummy smashed her nose,' says Billy, before throwing down a card and shouting 'Uno'.

'But the doctor said it was a good break, didn't he, Dad?' says Austin.

Nathan steps back and indicates for Alison to come stand beside Laura.

'Oh, Laura,' is all she can say as she nears her, noticing now the graze against her forehead and chin. 'I'm so sorry to hear about all this. I'm so sorry about... about Leni.'

Laura opens her eyes and stares at Alison for a few seconds, then frowns.

'Wait. What happened to Leni?' She cranes her neck so that she can see past Alison's shoulder. 'Nathan?'

Nathan throws Alison a loaded look then smiles at his wife.

'She's at home studying, remember? She's got a test tomorrow.'

Laura stares into space for a moment, then nods. She gently touches her bandaged nose.

'I don't remember a thing about today. Weird. I can't even remember why I'm here. Do you know?' Her hazel eyes stare up at Alison, who doesn't know what to say.

Nathan catches Alison's eye and indicates with a slight jerk of his head towards the doorway.

Austin watches them as they leave the room, his face deathly serious. 'We're here to make Mum feel better,' he says solemnly.

Alison pauses in the doorway and forces a smile at both boys.

'Well, I'd say you're both doing a great job of it.' She glances at Laura who watches her with tired eyes. 'Sorry. I just need to make a quick phone call,' she says, holding up her phone and stepping out the room, where Nathan awaits her.

'What's going on?' she asks Nathan. 'Why can't she remember?'

Nathan sighs and rakes a hand through his thick, brown hair.

'She hit her head pretty hard. The doctor said it's temporary amnesia. It's a blessing right now, while we don't know where Leni is, but they said her memory can return at any given moment.' He sways on his feet and swears beneath his breath. 'I don't know what to do. My parents are coming here soon. They're going to take the kids home for a few days. Laura's parents just left. I didn't tell any of them about Leni. I didn't want to worry anyone, but I'm going crazy with worry. I want to get out there and search every street, every house, every car.' His eyes grow red and shiny with frustration.

Not one for physical affection, and not good at dealing with emotional outbursts, Alison reaches out and pats Nathan on the arm three times.

'Look, maybe there's... there must be an explanation for all of this. Maybe Leni's gone off with a new friend for a few days? I used to do that as a teen.' *All the time,* she thinks. Home hadn't been the safest of places for Alison growing up.

Nathan nods. 'Of course,' he says. 'Yeah. It's likely that,' he says, although she can tell that he doesn't believe it.

'Rory said something about Michael,' says Alison, her heart pounding.

Nathan stares at the ground for a few seconds then looks up.

'Yeah. Her blood was found all over his hands and inside his house. He had her phone too.' Nathan's face reddens while he speaks. His fists clench and unclench. 'He says he doesn't know where she is, that she was at his place last night and cut herself, but... I just don't know. None of this makes sense.'

'There'll be an explanation to all of this,' Alison says, feeling uneasy. 'You'll see. She'll come home and you'll be angry that she ran off, but she'll be safe and well, and you'll all be okay.' She stops there. She doesn't know what else to say.

'I'd love to believe you,' says Nathan, his head down.

Behind him, Alison can see Nathan's parents rushing down the corridor towards them, their faces pale.

'Alison,' he says. 'Answer me this. What teenager can live without their phone?'

The truth of Nathan's words hit Alison hard.

He is right.

Does this mean what he is implying? Does this mean that Leni is in danger? And that Michael has something to do with it?

Alison feels the corridor spin. She can't go back in to face Laura. Not when she knows she's responsible for this mess. Not when she was the one who pushed the stupid key party rules on everyone and made it happen.

You're an idiot. Ugly. Stupid.

She bites her tongue so as not to shout 'shut up!' at her dead father in front of everyone, and quietly backs away while Nathan buries himself in the open arms of his mother and father. She hurries down the corridor, back down the elevator and exits the hospital on the ground floor. In the carpark, humid electric air and dark clouds promise a storm. The tiny hairs on the back of her neck stand on end.

A sudden desperate need to get back to her children seizes her. She needs to feel them in her arms and she needs to speak with Rory. Needs to hear from him that everything will be okay. She also needs to put her makeup on and make everything right again, make her dad's voice disappear.

Purposely avoiding her reflection in the rear-view mirror – she has no time for her father's crap right now – she reverses out of the parking bay and quickly exits the carpark, her foot heavy on the accelerator and her mind heavy with thoughts of Leni.

Please let her be okay.

Please let her be alive.

The phone rings while she drives. Rory's grinning face flashes up on the screen – it's an old photo, from their first wedding anniversary. Happier times, she thinks sadly.

Alison pulls over just as the heavy clouds finally burst with rain. With the wipers swishing back and forth across the windscreen, she dials Rory back.

He answers on the first ring.

'How's Laura?'

'Okay. She doesn't remember anything, not about Leni or Michael. I don't even think she remembers... err... Saturday night. Which is probably a blessing.'

'Okay. Well. The police have been and gone. They took Michael to the station and then dropped him back home. He came over to talk.'

'What?' Alison raises her voice to be heard over the rain lashing against her car. 'You didn't let him in, did you? How are the kids? Is he gone now?'

'Relax, the kids are okay. You're not going to believe this, but he told me that Leni came to his door last night. She was wobbling on her feet and barely holding a half-drunk bottle of Jack Daniels. He let her inside, out of the rain, and she dropped the bottle. It smashed into pieces and Leni cut her feet on the broken glass. Michael patched her up and let her sleep on the couch, because she'd begged him not to make her go home or ring her parents because she said if he did, she'd run away and nobody would ever see her again.'

'What? And you believed him? What about the phone?'

'Apparently she left it behind. He woke up at 5am and she was gone. He hopped into the car and drove around looking for her until it was 7am, and then he pulled into the driveway and fell asleep. He'd had a few beers before she'd shown up drunk at his door so he said he was dog-tired.'

Michael's story is starting to make sense.

Alison breathes a sigh of relief that Michael is not some kind of sick serial killer and hopes that Leni is just hiding out with a friend.

'Have the police found her yet?'

'Not yet. But Michael has nothing to do with it. He's been cleared pretty much. The police think she's run away. That she might be going through an emotional time.'

Alison thinks of Leni out there alone in this weather, without her phone.

'What about Tristan?'

'He hasn't heard from her. He's not coping. And Sam is hysterical. I saw Orlando before and he said that Sam got a handwritten note in the mail addressed to her that said "fucking slut" in red pen.'

'What?' Alison sucks in a deep breath and watches the world around her blur through the rain while the sky grows darker. 'Hey, I'd better go. This rain's getting worse and I just want to come home.'

'Drive safe,' says Rory, before adding, 'I love you, Allie.'

As she tackles the wet roads, Alison wonders who would have written such a note. She wonders if Nathan and Sam had slept together on Saturday night. It seems probable, now that Leni has gone AWOL. The poor girl probably found out and is likely traumatised by the idea of her father and Tristan's mother sleeping together.

But Nathan and Laura have always seemed like such a solid married couple. And though Alison had given Michael a hand-job, something she found increasingly disgusting by the minute, she hadn't been able to stomach sleeping with someone behind Rory's back, no matter how annoyed she'd been with him at the time. She's glad now that she hadn't, even though she regrets doing anything at all.

While she navigates the car through increasingly thicker traffic, she thinks about Sam, and Nathan, about everybody on the street, including her husband Rory, and wonders if you ever truly know anybody.

Though she knows that Rory and Naomi had disappeared out into the backyard on Saturday night, she'd guessed that they hadn't slept together. She just doesn't think her husband is the cheating type. But what she doesn't know is whether her husband has been thinking about Naomi since that night, if he's been fantasising about her beautiful dark skin and shiny raven hair.

There is no way that Alison will ever know, and she isn't sure how she feels about that.

But one thing she does know.

It's all her fault.

# 29

## *Tristan*

'Hey, mate, there's something I need to tell you.'

Tristan tears his eyes away from his phone – which he's been watching very closely as he waits for Leni to text him back, so closely that his eyelids feel like sandpaper every time he blinks – and looks at his dad.

His dad shifts around on his feet, passing his keys from one hand to another as though nervous.

'It's about Leni.'

Every part of Tristan's body turns cold, except his heart – which flutters to life in his chest.

Tristan feels strange, like he's experiencing an out-of-body experience. Like the world has stopped turning and has left him spinning.

The look on his dad's face isn't right. Too pale where his olive skin usually glows. He watches as his dad shoves his car keys in his jeans pocket and rests a hand against the bedroom door frame.

'Well. It seems as though she hasn't been in contact with her family for over twenty-four hours... except for one text to her mum. But that's it. She didn't even sleep at home last night.'

Tristan releases all the air that's been trapped in his lungs, a breath he feels as though he's been holding onto since Sunday.

'I thought she was ignoring only *me*,' he says after about half a minute of silence. His stomach twists. But now he'd rather that. He'd rather that Leni was still talking to her family and maybe just annoyed at him. It's better than her being somewhere out there, alone or with some lunatic, or in some kind of danger.

He wants to leap to his feet and race out the room and begin his search for Leni, but the look on his dad's face has paralysed him.

'Mate, they think that something may have happened to her,' he says, his voice trembling. 'Foul play. Her phone's been found. And there's blood.'

Tristan feels like the bed beneath him is falling away, and the floor, the house, the earth... everything. Nothing is solid anymore.

He can't speak. There are so many questions but he can't manage to coax them down the pathway from his mind to his mouth.

'Michael had her phone. He's been taken away and questioned by the police.' Orlando crosses the room and peers through the blinds of his son's window. 'Oh, Michael's standing on his front lawn, so he's back.' Orlando shrugs. 'I guess the cops mustn't think he did anything wrong.'

Tristan finally shakes his body free of the strange paralysis that had afflicted him and springs from the bed.

'Don't get any ideas, mate,' says Orlando, blocking the bedroom doorway, but Tristan's anger floods his veins and muscles with a superhuman strength and he easily shoves his stocky dad aside and charges down the hallway.

He needs to know where Leni is. Right now. He needs to know if anybody has hurt her. Because if they have, they are going to die.

Bursting out onto the darkened street, black and glossy from the recent rain, he crosses two lawns to get to Michael's house.

Michael isn't standing out on the lawn like his dad said a moment ago, so Tristan bangs on the front door and, after hearing some kind of sweeping sound, Michael finally opens the door.

'Don't step inside, there's glass everywh–' Michael says stepping back, his eyes wide, unprepared for Tristan who crashes against him and pins him against the wall.

'Where, the fuck, is she?'

'I don't know where she is, mate. I don't know,' says Michael, palms up.

'Why did you have her phone?' Tristan twists Michael's crumpled shirt collar around his red-hot, trembling fists.

'She left it here, mate. She slept here last night. She'd been drinking and crying. I'm not lying. Suddenly she was gone and I drove for hours trying to find her.'

'She would never have left it behind. Not her phone.' Tristan can feel his power withering by the second and despite still managing to keep Michael pinned to the wall, he has a feeling that if Michael chose to, he could easily overpower him.

'She did. Trust me. I would never hurt Leni. But she is hurt. She was drinking and dropped a bottle. That's why there's blood and glass everywhere.'

Tristan relaxes his hold on Michael, uncoiling his fists.

'Why was she drinking?' he asks quietly.

'I think she's going through something. It's not my place to say what,' says Michael, looking away. 'You need to speak to your mum.'

'What do you mean?' Tristan is thrown. What on earth does his mum have to do with Leni drinking?

'Just tell me what it is. My mum's not home. She's gone to the hospital.'

'Has she gone to see Laura? Do you know how she's doing?'

'No. I tried calling Mum before but she's not answering. She's been acting weird since Saturday night.'

'Your mum?' Michael sighs. 'Yeah, well, that's why you need to have a talk to her when she gets home. You should find this out from her, not me.'

'Find what out?' Tristan's voice comes out hysterical. He feels like he is going to lose his mind. 'Just tell me. Leni's life might depend on it. Please. I need to find her.'

Michael's eyes shine with pity and perhaps concern, as Tristan releases him.

'Okay. Well, on Saturday night, your mum and Leni's dad, Nathan, well...' He pauses and raises his brows, rubs at his chin. 'Leni walked in on the two of them...' Michael's voice trails off. 'I'm sorry, mate.'

Tristan stares at the blank wall beside Michael's head, as though there'll be something written there, an explanation to the crazy talk that has just spewed out of Michael's mouth.

'Wait, you're saying that Leni saw *my mum* with *her dad*?' Tristan takes a step back. 'What the actual fuck? Seriously. What the–'

Michael puts a hand on Tristan's shoulder and grips it firmly.

'Can I make you a coffee, mate? Or a tea? Something to calm your nerves.'

Tristan pushes his hand away as the fury from a few minutes ago returns. He steps back again, away from Michael and towards the front door, glass crunching beneath his sneakers.

'For all I know you've probably hurt Leni, done something to her, and you're lying about my mum to cover up. I know you've always been in love with her.

Everyone on the street knows about your sad, pathetic obsession with my mum.'

Tristan backs his way out the front door, trips on the doorstep while Michael stares at him as though *he* is the crazy one.

'Stay the fuck away from us, you fucking freak. Just stay the fuck away.'

# 30

## *Leni*

Leni can't get the image out of her head, of Sam – Tristan's *mum* – whom she's grown so close to over the years that Leni almost looks to her like a second mum, grinding her hips against Leni's half-naked *dad.*

She shakes the opened bottle of pills she stole from Michael's cabinet and gets the mini bottle of tequila she'd swiped from his kitchen ready to chase the pills down with, and swallows another two – her ninth or tenth? Her head feels fuzzy and light. She can't actually remember how many she's taken.

A cool wind snakes its way through the park and sends the dry wisps of her long, damp hair dancing around her shoulders. Strangely, she can't feel the cold, just the roughness of the bark from the tree she is leaning against. It keeps poking through her shirt and itching her back. She can also feel the wetness of the grass beneath her, seeping through her jeans.

Her hands and feet throb, the cuts from that bottle she'd dropped have dried up and stopped bleeding, thank God, but they still hurt. She wants to die.

The absence of her phone is strangely both good and bad. She feels lighter. Weirder. As though she's forgotten something. But ultimately, she feels free. It's as though leaving her phone behind has severed her connection to the rest of the world.

To Tristan.

A horrible sinking feeling collects in her chest when she thinks about her boyfriend. She wants to go to him, to explain, but how is she ever going to face Tristan now that she's seen Sam and her dad having sex? She'll never be able to tell him. She can't do that to him. He loves his mum so much. Leni has never seen a boy so close to his mum. He's close to his dad too. They are like best mates. This is going to break him. It'll break the whole family if everyone finds out.

Better to stay away and take her secret with her to the grave. Or maybe the pills will just damage her brain enough so that she can forget what she'd seen. Forget that the world is a dark and sinister place where bad things happen and nobody is who you think they are. And then she can continue on her merry way with Tristan and life, oblivious to what has happened between Sam and her dad.

Her dad. She hates him right now. How could he have done that? How can he betray her mum like that? Her mum is the best mother and wife. Does everything for them all. And what does she get in return for all of that? A cheating husband. A *snake.*

Leni wonders just how long Sam and her dad have been having it off. They kept apologising after she'd started kicking them and screaming at them to get out of her bedroom. They kept defending themselves by saying it was the first time, that it had never happened before, and that it will never happen again. Sam had even threatened to kill herself.

Leni had screamed back at Sam to go and do it before she'd kicked them out of her bedroom.

Tears roll down Leni's cheeks.

She's always liked Sam.

She swallows another two pills and realises that she is starting to feel a little numb. Her clothes are still wet, but she can't feel them against her skin anymore. It's strange.

Thunder cracks loudly somewhere nearby and the park lights up as flashes of lightening penetrate the dark night. She feels rather relaxed about it all when usually storms freak her out.

She smiles to herself. Everything feels almost warm and fuzzy now, as though she's been wrapped up in a fluffy blanket.

Things don't seem as bad.

She still wants to die though.

But at least she feels a bit better about doing it now.

She blinks and throws a hand to her face as headlights light up an otherwise empty carpark across from her. The lights blind her and she slides down, sideways, to avoid the blinding glare, and curls up at the base of the old Moreton Bay tree she rests against, the gnarled old roots cradling her trembling body.

Voices call out.

'Are you alright?'

They say something else. Two different voices. Two men.

Leni can feel the tablets frying her brain, sizzling her thoughts. She can't quite make out what they're saying to her as they move in closer.

When she opens her eyes, she can see a large pair of boots in front of her face as a man crouches down.

A tiny part of her mind, the last rebellious braincell that isn't dead yet, instructs her to run.

But she can't. Her body doesn't belong to her anymore. It's no longer connected to her brain.

The voices start up again and she still can't make out what they're saying. But something they keep repeating again and again... it sounds very familiar.

She thinks it's her name.

# 31

### *Aiden*

'Leni?'

'Shit. Aiden, call your sister.' Jakov bends down to scoop the unconscious teenage girl up into his strong arms. 'She's soaking wet and out cold,' he says, his breath short and sharp. 'But she's breathing, thank God.'

Aiden runs to the car and opens the back door, and while Jakov easily and very carefully lays Leni across the back seat of his car, he dials Naomi on the phone.

Rain starts to fall, fat drops that smack noisily against the roof of the car and the top of his head.

'Aiden?' She answers on the third ring, her voice low and groggy. 'What's the matter? It's past midnight.'

'We've found Nathan and Laura's kid. Leni.'

'What?' She's silent for a few seconds. 'Where is she? Is she okay?'

'She's okay. A little out of it, but okay I think.'

'How is she? Oh my God!'

Aiden hears her whisper, 'Thank you, thank you,' away from the phone. 'Where are you? Where did you find her?'

'She was in the park all wet and out cold. Taking some pills by the looks of it. She reeks of booze too. We're taking her straight to the hospital. She might OD... shit, I don't know. Just call Nathan and Laura.'

'Laura's at the hospital already.'

'What? How does she kno–'

'She doesn't. I'll explain after you get her there safely. Ring me as soon as you do. I can't leave the kids otherwise I'd drive there right now. I'll call Nathan. Then I'll see if I can get David's mum over to mind the kids.'

She hangs up.

Aiden sits in the back with Leni's damp-haired head resting on his lap while Jakov gets into the driver's seat.

'Drive safe, love, this weather's shit,' he says, staring out the window as the rain comes down harder and the reflection of the streetlights glint against the slick roads.

He feels for Leni's pulse and sighs with relief when he finds it, faint but there.

Naomi had told him about Leni going missing and he'd felt pretty bad for Nathan and Laura.

And although he's happy they found the girl; he worries now that they may have found her too late.

What if she has a seizure? What if her brain overheats?

They need to get her safely to hospital.

'Lucky we drove this way home, hey?' Jakov calls over his big shoulder. 'I mean. If we hadn't have heard about that pile-up accident on the main street on the radio, we wouldn't have come this way.' He stares at Aiden through the rear-view mirror. 'You know what this is,' says Jakov with that certain look flashing in his blue eyes.

Aiden smiles at his husband, who is obsessed with the idea that although deceased loved ones cross over, they never actually leave our sides.

'Yeah. I know. Your old man looking out for us, looking out for Leni.'

'You know it,' says Jakov, reaching out between the seats with his free hand to take Aiden's.

Aiden relishes the warmth of his lover's fingers. So real. So wonderfully perfect. So true.

Aiden loves Jakov for his beliefs. Sometimes his spiritual talk does Aiden's head in, but for the most part, he especially loves this part of Jakov. The Jakov that's always believing. Like a small, bright-eyed child believing in Christmas. Jakov believes in almost everything. Hopes. Wishes. Sees the good in everyone. Jakov is Aiden's shining light in what had been an otherwise dimly lit existence up until ten years ago.

'I love you,' Aiden says, eying his husband's half-face in the rear-view mirror, watching him while he concentrates on the dangerously slick roads.

'And I love you,' says Jakov, momentarily glancing over his shoulder into the back seat before a horn beeps and Jakov stares ahead then screams and slams on the brakes.

# 32

## *Jakov*

Jakov wakes to sirens ringing in his ears and people shouting at him that he is 'going to be okay'.

'Aiden,' he tries to say, but his voice isn't working or he can't hear himself speak. One of the two. He can feel tiny bits of glass biting into his skin and his chest throbs like somebody's whacked him across his ribs with a steel bar.

Blaring lights flash in his eyes and he blinks them shut.

Then suddenly he is being rolled onto a stretcher, cold air biting into his face, rain falling directly into his open mouth and his eyes, making them sting and his vision blur. His body jerks from side to side as he is lifted into an ambulance.

He can see a fire engine and a fireman cutting into his mangled car, orange sparks flying into the night.

'Aiden,' he shouts and this time he hears himself. Tears stream down his face as they hold him down and strap him in when he fights to get up and run to the destroyed vehicle.

'Aiden,' he says to the nurse who is leaning down and checking his pulse, her cold fingers pressing into his neck.

'He'll be okay. He's being freed any second now and he'll follow in the other ambulance. Trust me. We won't leave him behind.'

Jakov allows his head to fall back against the stretcher and closes his eyes to everything. Then he remembers Leni.

'Leni!'

'Who's Leni?'

'The girl. She was in the back with Aiden,' said Jakov, once again straining against his straps holding him down.

'She was thrown from the vehicle. They're still getting her down.'

'What do you mean?'

'Just close your eyes,' the woman says gently, her voice soft and soothing as he feels a tiny prick in his forearm.

Oh God.

Aiden... Leni...

Jakov starts to cry, a great big, heaving sob.

Until everything goes black.

# 33

## *Laura*

I wake up in hospital, my mother by my side and Sam sitting in a chair across the dimly lit room.

Tristan runs in and I blink. What is Tristan doing here?

'Leni's here,' he says, his eyes wide. 'Aiden. Naomi's brother.'

He's not making sense. But before I can ask him what on earth is going on, he races out of the room as quickly as he came.

My mother immediately jumps to attention as soon as I sit up. She gently rests her hands upon my shoulders and presses down.

'You're not going anywhere, love. The doctor said he will be back shortly, to let you know if you can go home.'

'What was that all about. Sam?' I ask. 'What did Tristan mean?'

Sam stands, her brow furrowing with concern.

'I'll go see. I'm sure everything's fine. I'll find out. Stay put. The doctors said no stress so let me find out what's going on before you start to panic. I'm sure everything is fine.'

Nathan comes bursting in before Sam leaves the room. I can't be certain, but I'm sure his brows raise just a tad and his eyes widen slightly when he meets Sam's questioning gaze. But then he turns his full attention to me. I swear those two are both acting weird. Almost as though they know something I don't.

'There's been an accident, Laura. It's Leni. Aiden and Jakov found her in a park. She'd taken pills. Then on the way to hospital they had an accident on the slippery roads and Aiden's in intensive care and Leni, Leni was thrown from the vehicle. She has a huge cut to her neck, and her back and spine have received bruising, but remarkably, she's alive.'

He squeezes my arm, his fingernails biting into my skin, reviving me out of this fog I've been existing in.

'She's *alive,* Laura,' he says, tears filling his eyes.

Despite my mum's protests, I stand. The room begins to spin, and before I can warn anyone, my stomach heaves and my mouth fills with saliva before I vomit at my own feet. I stare at the multicoloured mess on the floor and back up at Mum and Nathan. My head throbs and I press my cool hand against my forehead.

'Take me to her now,' I say, ignoring my mother's offers to go herself.

A nurse appears and after a bit of tutting and fussing, she quickly helps me to clean myself up and sends me on my way with Nathan to see Leni.

My head is fuzzy and light. I know I fell in Michael's driveway and hit my head – broke my nose. I know this because Nathan keeps telling me… but I can't remember the actual event.

And now he's telling me that Leni has been taking pills! That she has been in an accident no less.

This is all a dream. It has to be some kind of crazy nightmare.

Nathan holds my hand and leads me along the corridor, and we're nearly bowled over by Naomi who rushes past us, creases of sleep embedded in her cheek, her dark hair a tangled mess.

'Oh God, Laura. Leni. I'm so sorry. I need to see Aiden,' she says, before rushing down the corridor.

After taking the elevator and walking the length of two long corridors, Nathan guides me into a room filled with equipment that is attached to Leni via various tubes and wires.

I stare down at my daughter, at the cuts and scrapes on her face, at the thick neck brace she is wearing, and at the blood seeping through her bandaged hands.

This is not real. This cannot be real.

'She got the cuts on her hands from last night,' says Nathan, sounding very clinical, almost like a doctor. 'She was drinking bourbon and dropped the bottle at Michael's place and cut her fingers up on the broken glass when she'd tried to clean up.'

'What was she doing at Michael's?' I ask, still unsure as to why I was at Michael's when I fell. I do recall that Leni hadn't showed up to school that day and I had been concerned because Tristan hadn't heard from her either. But it doesn't make sense that I'd waste time by going to Michael's.

'I'll explain later,' says Nathan after sharing another brief but loaded glance with Sam.

I'm not sure that I like the atmosphere I'm picking up between the two of them. It seems intimate. As though they share something I'm not a part of.

But for now, I shove my insecurities and suspicions aside and ease myself into the chair beside my daughter's bed. This is where I belong.

Her hand is limp and cool as I gently lift it and cradle it between my own warm hands.

I press my lips to her fingertips, and they wiggle beneath my touch.

My heart warms and I smile as I stroke her cheek.

Leni is alive.

And for now, that's all that matters.

# 34

## *Naomi*

Naomi tries very hard not to stare at and read the disturbing story a child in her son's classroom has written, the boy's artwork sitting side by side next to her son's.

*'Scary man,'* it reads, along with painted blotches of red resembling blood.

She shivers and tries to concentrate instead on the work her youngest child, Sean, has created throughout his first term at school. He is a great little artist and she knows that David would have been so proud of him. She's already toured her other two children's classrooms and has viewed their work, and now it is Sean's turn.

Normally she takes her time carefully going over every little detail of her children's work, but she is finding it difficult to concentrate this time while her brother Aiden still sits in the intensive care ward in an induced coma right this minute. It's been a week. The doctors have suggested they'll bring him out of it soon, but they'd said that last week and in the end it didn't eventuate.

'It's wonderful work, Sean. Beautiful, in fact. You are super creative, sweetheart.'

She draws him into her arms and hugs him extra tight, closing her eyes to block out everything else and just savour the moment.

'Naomi.'

Naomi opens her eyes to see Laura coming towards her, her nose still in bandages and with her son, Austin, in tow.

'I'm about to go see Austin's work and was wondering if Sean would like to come too, then I can take all the kids out for ice-cream and bring them back to my place.'

Naomi swallows down the thick lump in her throat that had formed while she was hugging Sean and now just won't disappear. And it's only growing thicker at Laura's kind offer.

'That would be... I appreciate it, Laura.' Her eyes stray to Laura's plastered nose, her bruised eyes, and she can't help but wince. 'Only if you're up to it.'

Laura points to her nose and grins.

'Oh, this? I'm fine now. Apart from looking like I'm recovering from a nose job, I'm fine. I woke up my normal self, this morning.' She smiles softly. 'You know, everything is so much clearer to me. It's like after a week of moping about the house, a switch has been flicked.'

Naomi sweeps Laura into her arms for a hug. She loves her friend so much and just wants to cry. About everything. About Laura's situation with Leni... and her situation with Nathan. She wants to cry for Aiden, for Jakov. For David. She can't stop thinking about David lately.

Naomi quickly wipes away the few tears that have begun pooling in her eyes.

'Shit. I feel bad for falling apart when life's been so shit for you, Laura,' says Naomi, wondering how Laura is managing to appear so positive and sunny when she has a daughter recovering at home from a car accident and near-overdose, and on top of all of that she has to deal with the knowledge that her husband may or may not have slept with one of her closest friends. Naomi isn't certain how much Laura knows yet and is definitely not going to bring it up anytime soon. 'I'm here for you.'

'As am I. Now go and see Aiden. And please tell him he's got to wake up and get better in time for our wedding anniversary.'

Naomi stiffens.

'You're not still having that, are you?' She feels her cheeks heat up. 'I mean... sorry. That was rude of me. I shouldn't be so presumptuous.'

Laura shakes her head and smiles.

'Don't be sorry, please.' She shrugs. 'I know. I know. Why should we be celebrating? When my husband... well, he denies everything... but... I know how it must look.' She wrings her hands together. 'I've chosen to believe him. He insists they didn't sleep together and I feel as though he's telling the truth.'

'I am sorry, Laura. That was totally insensitive of me to say that,' says Naomi, regretting her words.

'No. No.' Laura smiles again. 'We're alive and Leni's alive and we're grateful and we're just wanting to put this nightmare behind us, the whole thing, and move forward. We're just focusing on the fact that Leni's okay. So, it is a celebration in a sense.'

'Sounds good,' says Naomi, giving Sean a quick side-hug and whispering 'I love you' into his ear before he joins Austin and Billy. 'The doctors seem to think that Aiden is responding well so I hope you're right. I really do hope that he wakes up soon. Fingers crossed. And you know what? Your wedding anniversary is going to be amazing!'

'Hope so,' says Laura, laughing. 'And hey, when your brother *does* wake up, you need to give him a big hug and thank him, and Jakov, for saving our girl.'

Naomi nods and can't help but ask, 'How's Michael? I've been meaning to see him. I heard about Tristan turning up at his doorstep and roughing him up.'

'He's okay. He understands Tristan was just upset about Leni.'

'How is he? Tristan, I mean. Do you know?'

'He's okay. But he's keeping his distance. He's worried about Leni. Worried that she doesn't love him anymore. So, he's keeping his distance until she feels better. They've been messaging though.' Laura's smile disappears and her eyes darken with worry. 'They're so sweet and have been through so much at their young age. I hope they stay strong and pull through. Their friendship is too precious to lose.'

Naomi smiles. 'I'm sure they will.' She sighs. 'Right. Okay, I'm off. Thank you so much.'

She waves at Laura and the boys, and rushes out of the classroom door, hoping that by the time Laura and Nathan hold their anniversary party, everything will be back to normal again for the whole street.

But as she pulls into the hospital, she pushes the party far from her mind. She has Aiden to worry about.

What if he never wakes from the coma? What if the doctors try it and he doesn't survive without the aid of the medical machinery he's connected to?

The idea makes her stomach swirl sickly and her head swim. She cannot afford to lose anyone else in her life. Not after David.

As she rushes down the long, never-ending hospital corridor and smiles at the nurses she's come to recognise, she hears Jakov laughing and chatting away and wonders who is in there with him, visiting Aiden. *Maybe Nathan*, she thinks. He did say he was going to swing by and visit despite Naomi warning him that there's been no change.

But when she enters the room, she freezes, mid-step.

At first, she is startled at what she sees.

Then she puts a hand to her mouth and stifles a cry.

'Oh my God! Aiden!'

There is her brother, blinking up at her, while he holds onto an incredibly ecstatic Jakov's hand.

'Hey,' he says, his throat hoarse. 'Sis.'

'This only just happened, an hour ago,' says Jakov, his eyes wide. 'And I didn't want to call you while you were at Parents' Day. I swear I was going to call in about another five minutes.'

'It's okay,' she says as she squeezes past Jakov, lightly touching his shoulders as she passes, and bends to give her baby brother a kiss on his smooth, dark forehead.

'Oi... steady on,' he says, his voice hoarse and his speech slow. 'I... heard it was... raining outside. You didn't have to... bring it in with you.'

She wipes at her streaming tears and laughs, then, with gentle fingers, brushes away the tears that had fallen onto Aiden's face.

'Oh, well, at least I know that you're okay. Ribbing me as usual. I was bloody worried.' She releases a shaky sob and goes round to the other side of the bed and takes her brother's free hand. 'I don't think I'll ever let you go.'

'Neither will I, so how's that going to work?' says Jakov, grinning whilst holding tight to Aiden's other hand.

Naomi exhales. Finally, she can breathe. She can dare to feel the joy that is growing inside of her and spreading from her heart outwards.

'Now... sit your butt down... in that chair,' says Aiden, speaking slowly but steadily, indicating the visiting chair on the other side of the bed. 'You can both share me.'

She smiles and does as she is told, and thinks again about Laura still wanting to hold the wedding anniversary party and although she'd initially thought a party, after what they'd all been through, absolutely absurd, she realises now that it is quite likely the only solution.

Rory comes to mind. She thinks about the uneasy conversation they'd shared when they'd crossed paths at the park last week, with kids in tow. She'd asked him how things were with Alison, genuinely hoping that they'd patched things up. Laura had mentioned how helpful Alison had been during all the chaos and how Rory and Alison seemed to be making a go of things.

But he'd clammed up and changed the subject, not meeting her eyes when he'd told her things were fine.

Naomi knew that this meant things were anything but fine but she isn't one to pry. She had merely let him know that she, like most of the neighbours on the street, were there for him, and for Alison and the kids. That if he needs a friend, Naomi's door is always open.

She made sure to stress that her door is open to Alison too, lest Rory get the wrong idea.

Though Naomi thinks that Rory is a wonderful man and she enjoyed the evening they spent chatting together, as well as the hug, she understands that he is a married man. She has already seen the damage the events of the key party has inflicted upon Laura and Nathan's marriage.

She likes Rory. Likes him even more after reading his heartfelt love letter to Alison. But she's going to lock her feelings away and respectfully allow Rory and Alison's marriage to mend, as Rory so ardently wished for in his letter to his wife.

Naomi is not a homewrecker. She will forget about Rory and move forward.

They all need to move forward and erase the past month with a fresh start. Erase that terrible night which seemed to be the beginning of everyone's troubles.

The worst, she thinks, as she clings to her brother's hand, is finally behind them.

# 35

*One month later*

***Laura***

'Make sure you come,' I say, still wearing my apron as I stand on Michael's front doorstep. I need to take a shower before everybody comes. At least I've done my hair and makeup already.

'If you think that it'll help to get everything back to normal, then yeah,' he says, smiling. 'I guess I'll be there.'

'Great. Nobody will say a word to you about what happened. I promise.'

I admire Michael. He's been unfairly judged for hurting Leni when all he did was take her in and give her a safe place to sleep when she was at her lowest.

If I, Leni's mum, can trust him, then I can't understand why anybody else in the group would still have reservations about him. Hopefully tonight will be the end of any negativity and the beginning of things getting back to normal for everyone on the street. Not just for Michael, but for all of us.

Leni and Tristan will have their first bit of time alone since Leni has healed from the accident... and from the events of *that* night. Well, not completely alone. They are going to be at the party with everybody else in the beginning, but after dinner is served, they will be taking all the kids to Tristan's for a movie night. It's all very cute.

I really hope that they get to patch things up, even if not as boyfriend and girlfriend. I just hope that they can remain close friends like they've always been to each other since they were little.

As I cross the street, I notice Rory and Alison out the front of their house. Actually, it is the shouting I noticed first.

My heart sinks.

Just when everyone in the street had thought and hoped that Alison and Rory had done a complete one-eighty, it seems as though Alison is back doing what she loves best – being an absolute bitch to her husband.

And Rory is sitting there and taking it as usual.

I think of what my mother has always told me – that people only treat you the way you allow them to. It's very true. I've been thinking about that saying a lot lately. Wondering about Nathan... rehashing over the way he's treated me lately. Wondering if we can actually turn things around for our marriage and focus on the future.

I'm not sure where to look as I near Alison and Rory's place.

'Is everything okay?' I ask, when Alison comes out to get something from her car. Rory is nowhere to be seen.

A willy wagtail perches on the mailbox and bounces across it three times before flitting away.

'Yeah, we're fine,' she says, looking highly irritated, but so beautifully made up.

I think about the Alison who visited me in hospital, the bare-faced one, and decide that I like her better.

But I watch *this* Alison lock her car and head back into her house and resolve to understand her a little better in the future. Alison was there for me when my life turned upside down. The least I can do is be there for her.

'Bye,' I call out, unsure if she can still hear me, and race inside, not to check on the finger food baking in the oven, but to slip into the new dress that Nathan had brought me last week – a guilt-trip dress I hadn't wanted to accept at first, but had done so in the end.

I had asked him if the dress meant that he'd slept with Sam but he'd put a finger to his lips and said that he was merely following the rules of the key party. Discussing that night would be pointless for everyone, he'd said, despite the fact that we'd already discussed it the night I returned from hospital. It was during that conversation that he'd assured me that he did not cheat on me and never would.

So here I am, staring at myself in the mirror, admiring the fact that I still have a decent figure and don't have too many wrinkles. I look good. And my husband has promised me that he'll never cheat on me.

Time to celebrate our marriage.

I laugh, almost bitterly, and shake my head at my reflection.

Somebody knocks on my bedroom door.

'Who is it?'

'Leni.'

I unlock the door to let my daughter in.

'Can we talk?'

'Yeah, come sit. I just need to put my earrings in.' I stick one blue-tasselled earring in while eying Leni from the mirror. My daughter looks beautiful, even with the few grazes that haven't quite healed and the one bandage across her neck – nobody would know that she survived being thrown from a vehicle so hard that she'd landed in a tree. 'Everything okay with you and Tristan? Are you guys back together again?'

'I don't know. I want to be. But every time I see him, I just feel angry…'

'Oh.' I pop the other earring in. 'Why are you angry at him?'

Leni doesn't meet my eyes.

'I'm not angry at him. I'm angry at...' Her voice trails off and she turns her head so that I can't read her expression.

But I know in my heart what she's going to say. She's hardly spoken to Nathan since the accident, and when Sam arrived at hospital one day, clutching a box of chocolates for Leni, my daughter had ordered her out of the room with a ferociousness I'd never witnessed in her before.

At the time, when I'd asked her what was wrong, and to please explain, she had begged to be left alone. She explained that it was private and she'd share it with me when she was ready.

I wonder if that time has come.

To have the conversation that I've been dreading all along.

'Is there anything you need to tell me, Leni?' I ask, while I stare at my reflection in the mirror. The healthy flush in my cheeks from rushing around earlier is gone. Now I look pale and ill.

'No. It's not something I should tell you.'

'Okay. But there is something I *should* know?'

Leni gets up and without saying a word, hugs me from behind.

'I love you, Mum.'

Tears fill my eyes and I turn and take my daughter into my arms.

'You deserve a great night tonight,' she says, drawing back and smiling down at me – she's a head taller than me now. They grow up so fast. 'I want you to have the best time because you deserve it.'

'Oh, thank you, darling. I *will* have the best time. I've got my family and my friends all under one roof tonight. Nothing could be better.'

Leni grins and I tickle her beneath her chin, her skin so soft.

'That's my girl. Now, let's go downstairs and have a great time. Honestly it's going to be the best night.'

'The best?'

I laugh nervously.

'Maybe just a great night. We could all do with a great night.'

Leni smiles and heads for the door.

'Okay. I'm going to text Tristan. And get ready.'

'Good. But remember what your doctor said. You've been through heaps, so you still need to rest and take it easy. No stress.'

'I hope so.'

'Promise me you'll come to me if you're feeling sad or upset, Leni.'

I feel a twinge in my heart as I watch my daughter's beautiful face wince slightly.

'Yeah, I promise,' she says. But she doesn't meet my eyes and I can't help but want to take the burden away from her little heart. Even though I know it's going to destroy my own.

# 36

### *Rory*

Rory's heart beats in time with the music playing – a fast song with rapid beats, something the kids are listening to – when he sees Naomi approaching him. He initially thought he'd been clever by hiding out in the darkest corner of Nathan and Laura's yard so that nobody at the party would notice him, or the bruise on his forehead. And for the past half an hour he'd gotten away with it, watching the kids play on the climbing frame and occasionally helping the little ones down the slide.

But here is Naomi, smiling wide and coming his way. He hasn't spoken to her, alone, since a few weeks ago when he'd turned up at the park at the same time as Naomi and her kids. What had followed was an awkward exchange where she'd offered to be a friend to lean on should he need it. And although it had been a lovely, kind offer, it had only served to make him want to run a mile.

The way her dark eyes had pursued his, for the truth about him and Alison, had felt intrusive. For some reason he didn't want anyone to know that his marriage was tough. He didn't want the world to know about his problems, least of all his neighbours... and especially not Naomi.

He wasn't sure what he wanted exactly, but he knew for sure that he didn't want any more trouble with his wife. That was something he was crystal clear on.

Across the yard, he can feel Alison's eyes on him and the stinging burn of her alcohol-fuelled fury.

'Hey, Rory,' says Naomi. 'How did you get stuck with kiddie duty?' She laughs, a cute squeak in her voice. He wonders if she's been drinking.

'Apparently, Leni and Tristan were meant to be the babysitters tonight but they're too busy *catching up*,' she says with a wink and a grin. 'Which, of course, is well deserved after what those two have been through.'

'Yeah,' Rory agrees, before taking a sip of his beer, which has gone warm in his hand. 'They're good kids. They've had a few rough weeks.'

'Yeah.' Naomi's eyes widen as she stares at the top of his forehead, at the bruise he's been desperately trying to hide behind his fringe.

His heart sinks. She's seen.

Here come the questions.

He just wishes that she'd leave it be.

'What happened to you?' She moves in closer and stares up into his face. She gently smoothes back his floppy curls and gasps when she spies the hideous bump beneath the bruising. 'Did… how did you get–'

Before Naomi can finish and before Rory can lie, Alison is at his side, looping her arm through his, drawing on her beer and glaring down at Naomi with her icy, observant eyes.

'I need a chat with my man, Naomi. You can excuse us,' she says, gripping Rory's arm tight.

Rory tries to shrug her away but she clings hard to his arm, digging her acrylic nails into his flesh. It is starting to hurt but he isn't exactly going to complain in front of everyone like a wimp.

'No, Ali, I'm having a chat with Naomi,' he says, his pulse whipping his eardrums. 'I'll talk to you later.'

He can see Naomi watching this exchange, concern widening her eyes, and by the look on her face, she's worried about him.

Rory feels bad for her. Her brother is still in hospital, awake now, yes, but still in rehab. The last thing he wants is for Naomi to get dragged into all his complicated crap with Alison.

'Okay, okay, I'll come with you,' he says, swearing beneath his breath before mouthing a quick sorry to Naomi.

'See, Naomi. I've got him trained well. What's that movie? *The Stepford Wives*? Except that he's a Stepford husband. Aren't you, Rory? My little Stepford husband.' She digs her nails into his bicep and he winces before he feels a tug on his shorts.

'Daddy, is Mummy being mean to you again?'

He looks down to see his youngest girl, Sal, staring up at him with big, innocent blue eyes.

Rory freezes.

'Mummy, you promised not to be mean to Daddy. You promised to never hurt him again,' says Sal.

At some point during his exchange with Alison, the music was turned down, and now several guests are starting to crowd around them. Parents are holding onto their kids, couples holding hands, united in the fact that they are watching a couple fall apart.

Rory feels the blood slowly drain from his head to his feet, leaving him shivering with cold.

'Well Daddy had better behave,' says Alison with a smirk, well aware now that they have an audience.

She finishes her beer then lets Rory's arm go, and stumbles forward, dropping the empty bottle in the process. The stubbie smashes, sending tiny dark green shards across the cream pavers.

Laura's mum swoops in, waving everyone away.

'Hey, kids, I think it's time I put a movie on for you all,' she says, smiling warmly at them all, her sparkling green eyes crinkling up at the corners.

Somebody crashes into some chairs nearby. Orlando. He is drunker than Alison, Rory thinks, shaking his head.

Laura comes to stand by her mum's side, Tristan and Leni in tow.

'Tristan and Leni, how about you guys take all the kids over to Tristan's place to watch a movie while this blows over,' says Laura.

Leni and Tristan link hands, smile at each other before they nod in unison.

'You can use my house, if you like,' says Naomi. 'The kids and I just hired a bunch of DVDs.' She shrugs. 'We still like going out to hire DVDs. It's something David liked to do. But, yes, you're all allowed to call us dinosaurs if you like.' She attempts a laugh, to lighten the mood.

Somebody calls out 'dinosaur' from the back corner of the yard and another laughs. People begin to talk amongst themselves again. Music fills the air once again.

It is then that Rory notices that Naomi has an empty glass in her hand. It had only just been full. She'd once told him that she drank only when she felt nervous or on edge at parties. Being an introvert, she said that she mostly liked to stay home and drink endless cups of tea.

He watches as Naomi hands Leni the key to her front door.

'Thank you,' Laura mouths at Naomi.

Rory's kids stare up at their dad, concern widening their round blue eyes, while Leni ushers them away.

Rory never wants to be looked at like that again by his kids, with such pity.

Though the music has started up again and people are making an effort at small talk, Rory can feel their eyes and thoughts tuned in on him.

He swears beneath his breath.

Great. Now Naomi is staring at him with the same pity-filled eyes his kids had regarded him with.

This is what he's become.

He pushes his way through the crowd, thinking how crazy it is that he and Alison had been getting along so well these past few weeks. But how earlier this week, on the anniversary of her father's death, it's like a switch has been flipped. He asked her to open up to him about her dad. But it had only served to clam her up even more. And here they were back to square one.

Naomi calls after him, her voice soft and silken, like the velvet sky above him.

Alison shouts after him too, calling him every name under the sun. A chair skids across the ground. His wife must have fallen because he hears somebody shout, 'Taxi.'

Normally, he'd rush over to help her to her wobbly feet. Not tonight.

Storming out the side gate, he crosses the crunchy, damp, front lawn to his house. When he arrives at his front door, he takes the key out from under the mat.

'Wait. Roooory.'

It's Naomi, her voice a caress in the darkness, even now when she's under the influence, her true caring nature comes through. Rory has always believed that mean drunks are just mean people drunk. Alcohol just strips any masks away.

Rory feels his throat thicken. He doesn't want to cry. Not now. Not in front of Naomi. *Fuck. Fuck. Fuck.* He fumbles with the key, trying to get it into the lock.

But when her warm hand slides over his shoulder, he stops what he is doing, sighs, and turns to stare into her dark eyes.

He wants to hold her, in his arms like that night. He's relived that night inside his head at least a thousand times.

And he wants her to hold him. So badly. He wants to feel the touch of a woman. A woman who cares.

She steps towards him, on wonky feet, and takes his trembling hand into her own.

Then she puts his palm against her cheek and turns her face slightly to press her lips into the palm of his hand.

He swallows and draws her in close, releasing her cheek and wrapping his arms around her small waist and pressing her against him. She smells like vanilla and cinnamon.

'I want you, Rory,' she whispers, sliding her hands up and down his back. 'I know it's wrong and I know you're married. But I just want you so bloody bad. And I want you now.' She shakes her head and frowns. 'But I won't do anything about it. I'll never do anything with a married man. But I just want you to know what I'm thinking about. What's inside my head... even though I won't do anything about it.'

Rory feels his body respond to the feeling of her warm body against his, but he still cannot bring himself to betray his wife.

*Something is wrong with me,* he thinks. Alison is right. I'm a Stepford husband. Programmed to serve only Alison.

And while she's my wife I'm never going to be free.

'Let's just hold each other, Naomi. I just wanna stand here and hold you like this.'

# 37

***Tristan***

'They're asleep, all of them,' whispers Leni, tucking a strand of her long, blonde hair behind her ear.

Tristan smiles and reaches out to his girlfriend and gently tugs her onto his lap. A warmth in his heart engulfs him as he hugs her tightly to his chest.

When he'd heard she been thrown from Jakov's vehicle, he thought he'd lost her forever. He still gets tears in his eyes whenever he thinks about it... the idea of no Leni in his life is unbearable.

'I love you so much,' he says into her hair.

She burrows deeper into his chest and clings tighter to him.

'I love you too, Tristan,' comes her muffled reply.

He kisses her forehead and she raises her head and kisses him on the mouth before snuggling back against him. It doesn't take long before she's fallen asleep. She still needs her rest, he thinks. Her delicate back is still bruised from the car accident.

He smiles to himself as he ponders his good fortune. Leni is alive. They are back together again, officially, as of tonight, and even though he will never forgive his mum and Nathan for what they have done, he will try to put it out of his head for Leni's sake. She'd told him earlier that she just wanted to forget it all. That her mum doesn't know and she doesn't want to hurt her. And so, he said he'd try his best.

For Leni.

After an hour of bliss, of cradling a sleeping Leni in his arms, she wakes and stares up at Tristan.

'What time is it?'

He looks at his phone.

'Eleven o'clock.'

Leni yawns. 'I wonder what time the party will finish. I'm so tired I just want to go to bed. My back's killing me.'

Tristan kisses her gently on the cheek and smiles at the sleeping bundles sprawled all over the floor.

'How about you do that. I'll stay up and watch the kids.'

'You sure?' she stares up at him. 'You are the best boyfriend in the world.' She yawns, gets up and bends down to plant a kiss on his forehead. 'I'll make you a quick video before I fall asleep.'

He laughs. 'What kind of video?'

She winks, the act extra seductive because of her sleepy, hooded eyes.

'A sexy one.'

'Um. Okay. I'll be waiting,' he says, grinning and shifting in his seat. 'But maybe I'll watch it *after* the parents come get their kids, and when I'm home.'

She grins, tiptoes her way out of the lounge room and when she reaches the hallway, she turns to blow him a kiss.

'Wait a second,' he says, getting up off the couch. 'I'll stand at the front door and make sure you get home safe.'

'Always the gentleman,' she says, before letting herself out the front door, the lawn wet and spongy beneath her feet as she crosses it and jogs across the road to her softly lit house.

Tristan watches her disappear through the front door and wonders how long the party will last.

He wonders if his mother will behave and if that bastard Nathan will keep his filthy hands off her. He thinks of Laura, Leni's beautiful mum, and cannot believe that his own mother and Nathan did that to her, betrayed her in the worst way. *And* his dad.

Tristan can't bear to think of his dad. He isn't even sure that he knows.

Taking out his phone, he sucks in a deep breath and quickly checks on the kids, to see if any of them are awake. But no, they are all sound asleep.

He needs to try to forget about what his mum and Nathan did. For Leni's sake. But it's hard. Especially when he visits at Leni's house, where Nathan struts around with a smug, sure expression on face. Tristan has fantasised punching it many times.

Tristan opens messages, sends a heart and a kissy face to Leni, and he wonders if he'll have enough self-discipline to wait until he is home after she sends her promised 'sexy' video.

A smile stretches across his face.

He is the luckiest boyfriend alive.

# 38

## *Laura*

Its only 10pm and I've already started clearing plastic cups and plates. Truth be told, after Alison's outburst at Rory, all the fun has been drained out of the party. I just want it over now.

Nathan has been staying away from Sam all night and I'm not sure what to make of that. I know that he is trying to make an effort to show me that he is fully committing to me and to celebrating our marriage. But at the same time, the fact that he's avoiding Sam is only serving to raise more questions for me. If nothing had happened between them, then there would be no reason why they couldn't act as friendly as they always have been with each other.

I wonder if the fabric of our marriage has a permanent tear down the middle of it now. Strangely enough, I feel as though Leni's accident has helped me to forge forward, to forget the past and focus on the now and how Nathan and I behave towards each other *today*. But it's the forgetting part that I'm finding difficult. And it's creating an invisible wall between Nathan and I, no matter how hard I try to push forward and focus on the future.

The kitchen bin needs emptying, so I knot the top of the bursting-full garbage bag and carry it out through the garage door to the big bin outside.

After dumping the rubbish, I lean against the bin lid and gaze up at the stars. It's peaceful out here, away from everyone.

I sigh at the simple beauty of the vast sky that I sometimes forget exists.

'Laura.'

I jump and turn.

'Oh, Orlando,' I say, hand on my beating heart. 'You scared me. I didn't even hear you come out.'

He stumbles forward, a drink sloshing around in his hand, and a wave of pity washes over me. Orlando hasn't taken the silence from Nathan and Sam on the matter of what occurred at the key party well at all.

'I saw you... and followed,' he says.

Blood seeps from a cut on his free hand.

'Are you okay?' I ask, wrinkling my nose at the smell of fresh vomit. A large wet patch blooms down the front of his shirt.

'Yeah, I cut myself pretty bad... trying to clean up the glass from... beer... Alison. But... I'm okay now,' he says.

The streetlights reveal huge, dark brown eyes staring intently at me.

'You know. I think the only way we can get over this... this thing with Sam and Nathan... is to... is to just you and me... you know. We need to do this, Laura. We need to fix it.'

I take a step back, my heel slipping between the pavers and making me momentarily unsteady on my feet.

'Orlando. We can't fix it. I know it's hard. I can't stop thinking about what if... what if they did do something. But we need to trust them as our partners.'

Orlando's face screws up and tears glitter in his eyes.

'They did it. I went through Sam's phone.' He runs a hand through his hair and then slides a palm down his face. 'There are messages. They slept together. Nathan keeps telling her not to tell me, or you. Sam wanted to fess up. She didn't want to hurt me, but she wanted to tell the truth because she felt bad.' Orlando's face turns red. 'But your bastard husband. Your bastard... Nathan...'

Everything stops in that moment, even my heart.

Nathan and Sam.

Though I knew it all along, instinctively, it still hits me like a kick to the stomach. Because Nathan *promised* he was telling the truth.

He *lied* to me. Stood in front of me and swore 'on my life' that he has never and will never cheat on me.

That's the part that is unforgivable. I'd rather he'd told me the truth. Because at least he'd be being honest.

Now... now he's broken my trust.

And like Alison's smashed beer bottle, my shattered trust is likely beyond repair. Because how do you repair broken trust?

'I'm sorry, Laura... I'm–'

'Just go home, Orlando. Leave me alone,' I say, my voice strangled.

Orlando sobs and my heart breaks to see the tears streaming down his face.

He needs help.

But I need to be alone. I need to absorb that one of my closest friends slept with my husband, and my husband slept with one of my closest friends. A double betrayal.

And Nathan lied about it to my face.

'I can't get over it. I can't, Laura,' Orlando says, reaching out to me.

Reluctantly, I allow him to cling to me while he cries, all the while my own tears refuse to fall, despite my throat tightening and my eyes stinging.

After a couple of minutes, I pull away, the stench of stale vomit once again filling my nostrils.

'I think you should go home and rest, Ollie,' I say, gently rubbing his back. 'Sleep it off. Everything will feel better in the morning.'

'What are you going to do?' he asks, his voice small, like a child's.

'I think I'll go in and shut the night down, to be honest, as I'm just dying to go upstairs to bed.'

Orlando sways on his feet. 'You want me to come with you? To bed?' He waggles his eyebrows and then his face collapses into misery again. 'Sorry. Bad time to joke.'

I sigh and shake my head.

'You need to go home now, Ollie,' I say.

Then I turn on my heel and leave him out there alone.

# 39

### *Orlando*

Orlando heads inside Laura and Nathan's house and stumbles upstairs, the steps swaying and seeming to shift beneath his feet. Somebody in the backyard told him that Laura had gone upstairs. He needs to find her.

He needs to apologise. He needs to apologise for what he'd said about Nathan and Sam. Sam doesn't know he's been through her phone and now she's going to find out from Laura and she's going to get upset with him.

There's no use in ruining both marriages, he thinks.

Maybe he can eventually block what happened out of his brain and move forward. Sam's been trying. He can try too.

He needs to find Laura and tell her he made it up. Then Laura can feel happy again. Then they can all be happy.

He trips and stumbles his way onto the second floor. So much for the party being over, he can still hear the music pumping from outside up here.

Once upstairs, he sees three doors. He's only been upstairs in this house once before and he briefly recalls the middle room being the one which Nathan and Sam had disappeared into that night. But he shakes his head and pushes Nathan and Sam from his mind.

Laura.

Find Laura. Apologise.

Then, after he's sorted things out with Laura, he needs to go home and sleep.

His eyelids feel so heavy. His body too. He needs to sleep for about a year.

Then he can wake up brand new.

He decides to try the door on the left as it looks like just the place for a master bedroom.

It's unlocked, but before he turns the knob, he puts his ear to the door. Somebody, likely Laura, is inside. Talking in a low, sexy voice.

He frowns in confusion.

Maybe she's changed her mind about getting revenge on Sam and Nathan.

Maybe she told him she was going upstairs to bed, so that he would follow her. So that they could have their revenge sex.

Blood flows from his addled brain down into his pants.

'I want to be with you. I want you to kiss me... I want you to hold me...' A giggle. 'I want you to...'

Orlando stumbles back a step and shakes his head again, trying to clear his head, trying to straighten up.

Laura wants to have sex with him. She's changed her mind.

Maybe this is the only way. The only way they can put things behind them. Make things right.

He stares at the door and the knob blurs and then comes back into focus. He's had way too much to drink and he worries that he might go soft in the middle of it all. But he isn't exactly going to turn down Laura, not when she needs him.

Maybe they can just kiss and cuddle, he thinks. It's not sex but frankly, he'll be happy with that. It felt so good to be hugged by Laura outside a few minutes ago.

The doorknob makes a tiny squeak as he turns it in his sweaty hand.

He stumbles in and remembers to shut the door behind him.

'Who's there?' comes Laura's voice. But it sounds as though she's trying to sound girly for him. Cute and innocent. Something glows on the bed, piercing through the darkness.

A phone.

He follows the screen's bright light and laughs. Maybe she wants to film them together. Who knows what kinds of other kinky stuff she's into?

'It's me,' he says. 'I'm glad you changed your mind. But we don't... we don't have to do it... we can just cuddle...'

'What?'

He climbs onto the bed and he feels her warm body stiffen at his touch.

'Get out of here,' she shouts, and at first Orlando freezes, but then he remembers that Laura said she liked it rough when they chatted on the key party night. Maybe... maybe she wants to act out a fantasy? Does that mean she wants him to take her by force?

It is dark and he can't see her face yet while his eyes are adjusting to the dimness of the room, but he can feel her warm body beneath his fingers, her bare skin. He wonders if she's naked.

'Oh shit, Laura,' he mutters, his heart racing. 'I've wanted you so fucking bad these few weeks.'

She screams. Loud and high-pitched.

The sound shocks him.

He wasn't ready for it.

Orlando puts a hand to her mouth, his bloody, cut-up hand which throbs against the pressure.

'Shit, Laura. Be quiet. We don't exactly want them all to come rushing in, do we?'

He laughs, his hand still pressing against her lips, his head spinning.

'I can't believe we're going to do this. Or at least attempt it.'

In the dark, his fingers find her underwear, the only thing she's wearing, something lacy and tiny. He tries to tug them down.

She screams again, the sound muffled beneath his hand, and she thrashes under him. Gosh, she is really putting on the act, he thinks.

'What made you change your mind?' he asks as he bends to kiss her.

He removes his hand and she screams again, right in his ear.

Screams the bloody house down.

That is when he blinks and realises that his blurry vision has finally adjusted to the darkness.

This is not Laura lying beneath him.

It is a teenage girl.

'Leni?'

He draws back. Horrified.

'Leni? Oh God.'

She continues to scream, her eyes wide with fright, and with Orlando's blood smeared across her face and neck.

He clamps his hand back over her mouth and feels instantly alert, as though every trace of alcohol has evaporated from his system in this single moment.

'Stop screaming, Leni. Please. I'm so sorry. I'm sorry, I thought you were your mum… I thought… oh God.'

After a few more seconds, her feels her relax under him, and he removes his hand and breathes out, hard and fast.

'I'm so sorry, Leni. I'm sorry, I–'

He pauses mid-sentence when he realises that she isn't just not screaming anymore, she isn't moving either.

Seizing her shoulders, he gives her a shake.

'Leni. Oh God, Leni. Wake up.'

She remains motionless and floppy.

His heart races in panic. What if he's killed her? What if he's hurt Leni? Leni, who's already been through so much.

Sliding off the bed, he presses his desperate, fumbling fingers against her wrist for her pulse, but fails to find it. He is useless at this kind of thing.

He backs away from the bed, just as the bedroom door bursts open, casting a yellowy light into the room.

When he sees Leni's illuminated form, passed out on the bed, he vomits.

'Tristan,' he murmurs to himself. His son is going to kill him. He is going to hate him forever. 'Oh God, Tristan,' he groans, his head in his hands.

The room fills quickly.

'What happened?' someone asks.

Orlando has no words.

He wants to sink through the house, through each floor, and fall into the earth beneath them and die.

# 40

*Now*

'She's dead.'

'What?'

'She can't be.'

'Why is she even… what's she even doing here?'

'It's her house, idiot.'

'You know… you know what I bloody mean.'

'She's half-naked.'

'Oh God. Oh God, the poor love.'

'Is that blood?'

'I'm going to be sick… oh shit… this can't be happening…'

'Check her pulse again.'

'*You* do it.'

'I can't feel anything.'

'Jesus, what is wrong with you? Oh… oh my God… she's… the poor thing. She can't be dead. She just can't,' says Samantha.

'Pull the blankets up. Give her some dignity,' says Naomi.

'I didn't know it was her,' says Orlando, his voice strained in anguish. He shakes his head as he backs away from the body and bumps into a chest of drawers, sending knick-knacks wobbling and a pink, glittery candle tumbling to the ground. 'I didn't know… I thought it was… I thought Laura was play–'

'Let me *through*,' says Nathan entering the room, his voice rising in anger. 'Oh God... oh shit... Get out of the way – now!'

'Give him some bloody room,' shouts Michael.

Laura appears at the bedroom door. She stares at the body for several seconds and then makes a sound, somewhere between a groan and a gasp.

Orlando flees the room.

Samantha vomits into her hand.

'No, no, no,' wails Laura, who now kneels by the bed. She begins to sob, at first almost silent, then loud and raw, her guttural howls escaping through the half-opened bedroom window and travelling down the silvery, moonlit street. A street that will never be the same again.

Downstairs, the autumn wind slams the front door shut behind Orlando, who stumbles as he runs across the lawn, fleeing the house as though it is burning.

Nathan follows.

'What have we done?' comes the aggrieved, low tones of Alison from a shadowy corner of the bedroom. 'Oh God, what have we done?'

Several minutes later, over the haunting wail of an ambulance siren, a single gunshot cracks into the night.

# 41

***Tristan***

Tristan watches Leni's video over and over again. He cannot believe what she has just sent. He also cannot believe what she *says* in the video. And she looks so beautiful lying in her bed like that, shirtless.

He was glad when Jakov returned from the hospital and arrived at Naomi's announcing to Tristan that he'd take over watching the kids so that he could go home.

Tristan had sent Leni back a little video of himself, also shirtless in bed, declaring his love for her in what he hoped had been a sexy or at least romantic reply.

But she hasn't messaged back yet. She's either fallen asleep or is making him another video. He hopes it is the latter.

When he'd walked home, earlier, he'd been tempted to climb the big tree in her front yard and knock on her window, but there'd been no light on so he thought it best to let her rest. And despite her sending the video, he realises that it has only been four weeks since she'd been thrown from the vehicle so he is going to try to take things super slow.

For now, they can just cuddle when they are together. He doesn't want to hurt her, pressure her or scare her away.

Tucked beneath his doona in bed, he continues to watch the video a few more times until he notices, through his bedroom window, that Leni's bedroom is lit up. She must be awake.

He gets up and stands by the window, hoping to see her, but instead he sees several shadows – people – moving about in her room.

A pang of fear flutters inside his chest. Has something bad happened? What are they all doing in there?

The front door bursts open and then slams shut.

Tristan races downstairs.

'Dad! What's wrong? Is Leni okay?'

But his father, who's olive skin has paled, races upstairs without a word.

Tristan opens the front door. He'll go over and find out himself. Make sure that Leni is okay.

But when he steps outside, he crashes straight into Nathan.

'Fuck,' Tristan says, stumbling back into the doorway. He feels his lip and tastes blood.

'You little fucking bastard,' says Nathan, shoving Tristan so hard in the chest he falls back and lands on his side against the first few steps of the staircase. 'It was you, wasn't it? And your dad is covering it up for you. I'm going to fucking kill you.'

'Why? What's happened? Where's Leni?' he asks, feeling dazed and confused. He's hit his head on the banister on his way down. Something warm drips down his forehead and into his eye. He tries to blink it away.

Where is his dad? He needs his dad to come down and help, but he is lost for words. Had Nathan found the video on Leni's phone? What on earth is going on?

A siren wails in the distance and grows louder as it draws closer. The sound sends his heart into a panic.

'Leni! I need to see Leni,' says Tristan, struggling to stand.

Nathan stands over Tristan and reaches down to yank him to his feet by his collar, his huge fist, raised, ready to punch him.

A gunshot rings out from upstairs, loud and deafening, freezing the looming fist in place.

Tristan gasps for air. He twists his head towards the direction of the stairs where his dad had disappeared.

With newfound strength, he climbs to his feet, shoves Nathan off him and runs upstairs, taking two at a time.

'Dad!'

He gets to his parents' bedroom and finds his father lying face down on the bed, a large red patch beneath his dark-haired head spreading, turning the white doona red. A gun rests in his now limp hand. Grandad's gun, from when he was a copper. Tristan was spanked once when his dad had caught him playing with it.

A loud, strange sound erupts in the room, so loud it brings Tristan to his knees – until he realises that it is coming from somewhere deep inside of him.

As he continues to wail and cry out *'Dad'*, he crawls over and onto the bed and takes the gun from his dad's hand.

Sobbing, he threads his fingers through his dad's unmoving ones and lies there, beside him, shaking uncontrollably, thinking that this moment cannot be real, despite it being the realest moment he's ever experienced in his life.

# 42

***Laura***

While I sit beside my sleeping daughter in hospital, I stare at my phone and read and re-read the same message I received from Ollie.

The last message I'll ever receive from Orlando.

*I'm so sorry, Laura.*
*I thought she was you.*
*I'm so sorry.*

A single fat tear drops onto the screen of my phone and warps the message.

I still cannot believe that Leni is here in hospital, again, this time for passing out after Orlando had mistakenly surprised her in bed. Orlando, who had confused Leni for me.

And I still cannot believe that Ollie is dead. That he died last night from a single gunshot wound to the head.

Self-inflicted.

Suicide.

Tristan is here too, getting stitches for having been knocked about by Nathan. Nathan had at first thought Tristan responsible for Leni's unconsciousness when it had been a confused and panicked Orlando all along.

I feel as though I'm trapped in a living nightmare.

Alison appears with two takeaway cups of coffees in hand. I'm still surprised to see this version of Alison again. The Alison from years ago, in the earlier years of her marriage. The Alison who visited me in hospital when I broke my nose over a month ago. No makeup and blonde hair twisted up and secured with a claw clip, wearing tracksuit pants and a baggy tee.

'Thanks, Allie,' I say, gratefully accepting a coffee.

'Oh, it's okay. That's what friends are for.' Alison wipes a stray tear from her eye and I realise that it is the first time I've seen her cry.

'Where's Rory?' I ask, but then I remember the fight at the party. Oh God, that feels like a year ago, not mere hours. Asking after Rory is the first thing that had come into my head and now, of course, I regret it. I'm not exactly thinking straight.

I reach out and take sleeping Leni's hand into my own, for strength, while I wait for Alison to compose herself.

'He's at home with the kids.'

Alison remains silent after that, while we sip our coffees, during which I go over and over my last conversation with Orlando. Had I somehow given him the idea that I was waiting for him upstairs?

No. No I hadn't.

But he was drunk. So very drunk.

I clutch Leni's hand tighter.

My poor baby has been through so much lately and now she is going to have to learn that Orlando has killed himself after realising what he'd done to her.

And then there is Tristan. That poor boy.

Sam has been inconsolable. The paramedics gave her something to put her to sleep, because she'd refused to let go of Orlando's body once the police had arrived.

'He's leaving me,' says Alison, cutting through the silence.

I meet Alison's blue eyes across the bed and make a noise in my throat, a sound of sympathy.

'I'm so sorry, Allie, I really am.'

'It's for the best,' says Alison. 'I haven't been the best wife.' She sucks in a deep breath and straightens her back. 'But I'm owning up to it. I'm going to get counselling and sort through some stuff. I want to be a better mum and... yeah, just a better person.' She drains her coffee cup. 'I've got so much stuff to sort out. Things I've locked away inside for far too long.'

I reach across the bed and take Alison's hand in mine. 'You can do it, Allie. I believe in you.'

Alison raises her brows and after a few seconds, draws her hand away.

'Yeah well, we'll see. I'm not sure that I deserve anyone to believe in me. Not after how I've been behaving.' She sighs and abruptly stands. 'Anyway. Time for me to go. Give Leni a big kiss from me when she wakes.'

Alison leaves the room.

I shift my gaze back to my sleeping daughter and bend to kiss her hand, feeling relieved that she is sleeping. A temporary reprieve from all the sadness she will face.

Leni's hand twitches and I watch as my daughter's dark lashes flutter against her cheek.

'It's okay, Mum. Everything's going to be okay,' Leni whispers, smiling, before she drifts back into a peaceful sleep.

Leni knows what happened between Sam and Nathan. She'd seen and that's why she'd reacted that way with the pills and the running away.

I sigh.

If Leni thinks everything can all be okay, then so can I.

Nathan and I are over. He doesn't know it yet, but I do.

Though I've been holding off telling him because of the trauma of the past twenty-four hours. I know that I will tell him soon. After Leni is home again. And after Orlando's funeral.

We can still bring up the kids together. The kids are what matters most to us both.

But I strongly feel that it's time to strike out on my own.

Find myself again.

Maybe get back into my art which I pretty much gave up after I met Nathan.

Like Leni said, everything's going to be okay.

# 43

*A year later*

***Leni***

Leni holds fast to Tristan's trembling hand. She is sure that any minute he'll break free and run back to his car, which is parked a street back.

Her eyes are immediately drawn to the 'For Sale' sign that is speared into the faded green lawn of Tristan's old house – it's been there for nearly a year, and she knows that Tristan can see it too. She feels his hand stiffen inside hers as the house comes into view.

Leni feels as though she is seeing the street, the same old street she grew up on, with new eyes – through Tristan's eyes.

It has taken twelve months for Tristan to return to the neighbourhood he once called home. To the place where his dad had taken his own life.

'Are you okay?' Leni asks, rubbing Tristan's arm. She can feel the hairs along his forearm prickle.

He nods, despite stopping in his tracks, his body rigid.

'Tristan? Is that you?'

Leni and Tristan turn their heads simultaneously to see Rory winding a garden hose into a coil, in Naomi's front garden, before making his way over to the white picket fence that separates him from them on the street.

He lets himself out through a small gate and approaches Tristan, putting a hand to his shoulder in the way that blokes do.

'How are you, mate?' he asks with a gentle smile and careful eyes.

Tristan seems to breathe for the first time since they'd arrived.

Leni sighs with relief.

Good old Rory. She's always liked him. He's always had such an easy, kind energy about him.

'I'm pretty good, thanks.' Tristan glances at Naomi's house and then at Rory, his brows slightly raised.

Rory smiles, the corners of his light blue eyes crinkling up.

'Yeah, it happened. Only just a couple of months ago. After Alison and I got officially divorced.'

'Oh. Wow. That's so great. I'm happy for you,' says Tristan. 'But... I mean. Sorry. Like, I feel bad that you and Al–'

'Don't say another word. It's all good.' Rory shrugs. 'Everything turned out for the best. The kids are happy. Alison is happy – well, as happy as she can be, she's making progress. We're great friends. And I'm...' He raises his eyes to the sky as though searching for the right word and when he finds it, he breaks into a huge grin and stares down at them both. 'Ecstatic!'

The sounds of a cheerful racket resonate from the backyard. There are a couple of cars in the driveway.

Leni smiles at the cheery sounds the kids are making.

'Hey, Aiden and Jakov are here. Do you guys want to join us for a barbeque?' asks Rory.

Leni meets Tristan's gaze and shrugs. A gentle breeze stirs her hair and she shivers when Tristan tucks a few stray strands behind her ear. His mere touch still has the same effect it has had since they first started dating – the ability to turn her legs to jelly and her heart into a jackhammer – in a good way.

'It might be nice. If you want to,' he asks her, his voice soft.

She nods.

Tristan smiles at Rory. 'Yeah, that'd be nice. Can we come in five minutes or so?'

Rory squeezes Tristan's shoulder. 'Take all the time you need, mate. See you both in a bit.'

Leni smiles. 'Thanks, Rory. See you guys soon.'

They watch Rory disappear around the side of the house into the backyard and turn to face each other.

Leni wraps her arms around Tristan and they embrace each other gently at first, and then more fiercely.

'I don't want you to let me go,' says Tristan. 'I don't want to see my house ever again. It makes me feel... horrible inside. I just want to be with you.'

'It's okay. We don't have to go to my place to hang out. I'm happy just visiting you at your new place. Well, year-old place actually.' She half-smiles. 'You don't ever have to return to this street again.'

Tristan wraps his arms around her even tighter and buries his face into her hair.

'I hate what he did to you. What they all did. I hate it so much. But I still love him. I still love him and...' Tristan's voice breaks and his body shakes. 'I just miss him so fucking much.'

Leni feels the world around her blur as her own tears form.

'I know,' she says, clinging to him tightly and rubbing his back. 'And that's okay. He was such a great dad to you.'

They hold each other like this for a long time, until Tristan draws back and smiles down at Leni, his face red and streaked with tears. He sniffs.

'What are you thinking about right now?'

Leni listens to the birds twittering in Naomi's tree.

'I'm thinking how out of all of this bad stuff, something good came of it. Like us – we survived it and grew stronger. And now Rory and Naomi.'

Tristan stares at Naomi's house and nods.

They both laugh when they hear Jakov growling at the children in the yard. Leni can picture the big man running after the kids, pretending to be a monster or a big bear, while they shriek and run from him.

'Yeah. Rory and Naomi are two of the nicest people in the street. I'm glad they found each other.'

'Let's never be mean to each other,' says Leni. 'I only ever want to be kind to you. I don't ever want to hurt you.'

'Same,' says Tristan, reaching down to stroke Leni's cheek in a tender way that makes her heart skip a beat. 'Sure, arguments happen, but as long as we always make up and never hurt each other in the process.'

'And we'll never part without saying I love you,' Leni says. 'My grandmother's famous advice.'

'She's a smart lady,' says Tristan, smiling, the setting sun lighting up his hair so that it sparkles like gold.

Leni takes his hand and gives it a squeeze. 'Let's go to this barbeque then.'

Tristan takes one last glance at his old house, his heart squeezing painfully for a second, and then nods slowly.

Together they both go through the little gate of Naomi's place and walk down the side of the house to the growing sounds of children's laughter and the delicious smells of good things being cooked on the barbeque.

And for the first time in a year, Leni feels the little sad, grey cloud that has hovered over her heart, lift a little, just enough to free up some of that joy that has been waiting patiently inside of her.

Leni laughs as Rory's boy, Max, a spitting image of Rory, races up and throws himself into Tristan's arms.

'Tristan!' he cries with glee. 'It's been fifty years!'

Everybody laughs.

Leni smiles and watches her boyfriend as the kids surround him and eventually drag him to the ground so that they can all pile on top of him.

'Hey, Leni,' comes a soft voice as an arm slips around her shoulders. 'It's good to see him back here again, isn't it? So good to have us all together again.' Naomi squeezes her while they watch Tristan and Rory and Jakov race around the yard with the kids in tow.

'Hey, Leni. Good to see you both,' calls Aiden, seated in his wheelchair beneath a lush green tree, a big grin on his handsome face.

'This is what life's about, Leni, isn't it?' says Naomi, her face beaming. 'This moment. That's all that matters.' She drags Leni over to where Aiden sits and takes both their hands in hers and squeezes them. 'This here. All of us together. This. Is. Life.'

'This is life,' says Aiden, his brown skin glowing, radiating happiness. 'And you've had one too many wines, sis,' he says, laughing. 'That's enough sentimentality for one day.'

'Oi, I've only had one. I'm just happy,' says Naomi, ruffling her brother's dark hair.

One of Naomi's kids shouts 'This is life' at the top of her lungs and then collapses into a fit of giggles on the lawn.

The setting sun casts a golden, apricot glow across the entire yard and softens everybody's faces.

Leni smiles as Tristan comes up from behind and hugs her to him.

She doesn't know what life holds for them in the future.

But she does know that this, right now, is enough.

'Yeah,' she says, running her hands up and down Tristan's arms. 'This is life.'

The End

# List of Characters

Laura – married to Nathan

Nathan – married to Laura

Leni – daughter of Laura and Nathan

Austin – son of Laura and Nathan

Billy – son of Laura and Nathan

Samantha – married to Orlando, best friend to Laura, childhood friend of Michael

Orlando – married to Samantha

Tristan – son of Samantha and Orlando

Michael – childhood friend of Samantha

Naomi – widowed mother of three

David (dec.) – Naomi's deceased husband

Matthew – son of Naomi and David (dec.)

Rory – stay-at-home dad of three children and married to Alison

Alison – married to Rory

Sal – daughter of Rory and Alison

Max – son of Rory and Alison

Dylan – son of Rory and Alison

Aiden – Naomi's brother, married to Jakov

Jakov – married to Aiden

If you enjoyed this book, please let others know by leaving a quick review on Amazon. Also, if you spot anything untoward in the paperback, get in touch. We strive for the best quality and appreciate reader feedback.

editor@thebookfolks.com

***Also by Vanessa Garbin***

THE LIES I TOLD HIM

YOUR EVERY MOVE

THE STEPS WE TAKE

THEIR LITTLE SECRETS

NO FRIENDS OF MINE

FOR MY OWN GOOD

LIES WITHIN ME

*Selected Titles*

**YOUR EVERY MOVE**

When young mother Dana discovers a bag of money under a bush, she thinks her problems may be over. Unfortunately, they are only just beginning. She starts to receive letters from someone claiming to be her "number one fan" and unless she complies with their bizarre demands, her family will be in danger.

*FREE with Kindle Unlimited and available in paperback!*

**THE STEPS WE TAKE**

A mother becomes increasingly at odds with her local community when she tries to deal with the bullying of her daughter at school. Yet her daughter is trying to handle it in her own way. When one bullying schoolboy goes missing, the family will have to reach the truth to remain together.

*FREE with Kindle Unlimited and available in paperback!*

**THEIR LITTLE SECRETS**

Sara's marriage is already under strain when her best friend's daughter disappears. With the parents acting strange, and her husband absent-minded and evasive, Sara starts suspecting they share a secret. When the body of a girl is found in a lake nearby, her resolve to solve the mystery will force her to question everyone she thought she knew.

*FREE with Kindle Unlimited and available in paperback!*

www.thebookfolks.com

Printed in Great Britain
by Amazon

40786942R00138